WAYNE STINNETT
and KIMBERLI A. BINDSCHATEL

Liable Charity

A Charity Styles Novel

◆ • ◆ • ◆

Caribbean Thriller Series
Volume 8

 DOWN ISLAND PRESS

Copyright © 2023
Published by DOWN ISLAND PRESS, 2023
Beaufort, SC
Copyright © 2023 by Wayne Stinnett

Library of Congress cataloging-in-publication Data
Stinnett, Wayne
Liable Charity/Wayne Stinnett
p. cm. – (A Charity Styles novel)
ISBN: 978-1-956026-61-0 (print)
Edited by Marsha Zinberg, The Write Touch
Final Proofreading by Donna Rich
Graphics and Interior Design by Aurora Publicity

To my great-grandson, Malakai Tomas Stinnett.
I've only met you once, but you've been foremost in my thoughts for the last nine months. You entered this world just weeks before this book was completed and I am already looking forward to one day playing, fishing, and swimming in the ocean with you.
Stay strong, Kai!

"Take chances, make mistakes. That's how you grow. Pain nourishes your courage. You have to fail in order to practice being brave."
–Mary Tyler Moore

If you'd like to receive my newsletter, please sign up on my website.

WWW.WAYNESTINNETT.COM.

Once a month, I'll bring you insights into my private life and writing habits, with updates on what I'm working on, special deals I hear about, and new books by other authors that I'm reading.

The Jerry Snyder Caribbean Mystery Series

Wayward Sons

The Charity Styles Caribbean Thriller Series

Merciless Charity
Ruthless Charity
Reckless Charity
Enduring Charity

Enduring Charity
Vigilant Charity
Lost Charity
Elusive Charity
Forced Charity

The Jesse McDermitt Caribbean Adventure Series

Fallen Out
Fallen Palm
Fallen Hunter
Fallen Pride
Fallen Mangrove
Fallen King
Fallen Honor
Fallen Tide
Fallen Angel
Fallen Hero
Rising Storm
Rising Fury

Rising Force
Rising Charity
Rising Water
Rising Spirit
Rising Thunder
Rising Warrior
Rising Moon
Rising Tide
Steady As She Goes
All Ahead Full
Man Overboard
Cast Off
Fish On!

Non Fiction

Blue Collar to No Collar

No Collar to Tank Top

Also By Kimberli A. Bindschatel

Operation Tropical Affair

Operation Orca Rescue

Operation Grizzly Camp

Operation Turtle Ransom

Operation Artic Deception

Operation Dolphin Spirit

Operation Wolf Pack

The Path to the Sun

You can find Kimberli at
WWW.KIMBERLIBINDSCHATEL.COM

The Gaspar's Revenge Ship's Store is open.

There, you can purchase all kinds of swag related to my books. You can find it at

WWW.GASPARS-REVENGE.COM

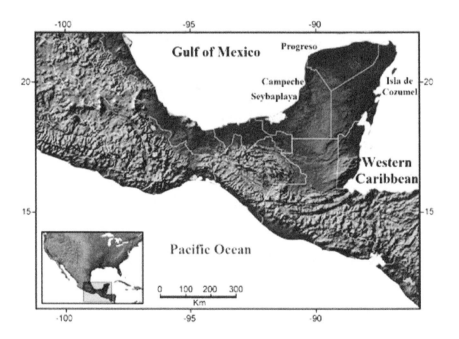

Gulf of Mexico

Progreso

Campeche
Seybaplaya

Isla de
Cozumel

Western
Caribbean

Pacific Ocean

0   100   200   300
Km

CHAPTER ONE

June 19, 2023
New Orleans, Louisiana

It was dark, nearly midnight, as a shadowy figure moved soundlessly along a vacant street. On both sides were dilapidated, mostly boarded-up houses. A single streetlight, half a block ahead, was the only illumination along the street.

Somethin' ain't right, the man thought, as his eyes bore into the shadows between houses and around the shrubs and trees that had been growing wild for years.

The mood feels off... Somethin' ain't right.

JP was always late, so he wasn't worried about that. It was just somethin' in the air. Like a bad odor but not really a smell.

There were enough bad smells in this part of town as it was—decaying wood in the dozens of houses that had been submerged during Hurricane Katrina and never repaired. The scent of rotting garbage, urine, and feces, all left behind by homeless squatters, floated near the ground like a dense, olfactory fog.

The man moved through the dark like the night creature he was. He'd always been able to slip around unnoticed, melting into the shadows. And he had one of those faces that nobody remembered.

All good assets to have for someone in his line of work.

But this feeling of paranoia was new. He tried to shake it off, focus on what he had to do, but the whole neighborhood seemed almost ghostly.

I'm the man, he thought.

He didn't have anything to worry about. He was on his own turf, and he was the boss. Even the two times he'd spent in the joint, his contacts afforded him certain privileges not given to most inmates. Chief among them was not becoming someone's bitch.

He spotted the abandoned house JP wanted to meet at—the back door was ajar. Most doors in this neighborhood had been kicked in by squatters or just left unlocked by whoever abandoned them. So, he wasn't surprised to find it open.

This area had been inhabited by mostly poor people without insurance before Katrina. Some fled elsewhere and never returned. Others died in their attics, trapped by rising flood waters.

Shit. Lately, every time I plan a meet, I know I'll be roustin' a buncha kids shootin' bombita before my buyer gets there. It's like I'm some kinda goddamn schoolmarm or somethin'.

Pausing outside the door, the man took a tube from his pocket and squeezed a small dollop of vapor rub on his finger. Then he smeared it on his thin mustache, twisting the ends up. He inhaled deeply. It had the desired effect, making him nose-blind to the stink he knew he'd encounter inside.

At least temporarily.

He kicked the door open and hollered, "NOPD! This is a raid!"

Ha-ha! That usually got 'em scatterin' like roaches. That is, if they weren't already sailin' off to oblivion.

Hearing nothing, he stepped through the doorway into the

2

gloom. He'd take it one room at a time, just like always, to ensure that no uninvited guests were at the meet.

When he was a kid, his uncle—the one who was a fisherman—had taught him the trick with the vapor rub. He'd also taught him that a red light doesn't ruin your night vision, so he always carried a little pocket light with a red filter over the lens.

He switched it on with his left hand, keeping his right firmly on the pistol tucked in his belt.

Stepping past the busted door, he thought the place sorta reminded him of the times he'd snuck back into his own home as a kid. The disarray before him even looked similar.

A fat rat ambled across the cracked linoleum floor of what had once been someone's kitchen. It stopped in front of the stove, looked over its shoulder as though annoyed by the man's intrusion, then moseyed on.

"Piss off," the man muttered after the rat, while scanning the rest of the room.

An empty matchbook and a glass ashtray, loaded with cigarette butts, lay on the counter next to an empty, forty-ounce brown bottle.

Why the recent squatters used an ashtray instead of just squashing the butts on the floor, he didn't know.

Some leftover sense of order, he thought, *the only thing left in their zombie brains.*

The man grinned at his own joke. *Ha-ha!, Zómbie Bombítas.*

Even with the smear on his lip, the odors assailed his nostrils. The smell was a mix of urine, mildew, and rot. Pretty much the same as in all the other houses in this neighborhood.

If another hurricane came, most of these old, abandoned houses would just be washed away—some were already starting to

3

cave in on themselves.

Yeah, another hurricane would be like urban renewal.

He stepped into the dining area, where there was an old table slanting toward the wall, one leg pushed in toward the middle like it was about to buckle. There was only one scarred wooden chair.

Around the corner, a little living room still had a couch, now ripped and covered in black mold. There was also a broken recliner, the footrest askew at an awkward angle. Under it, several more rats looked out at him with beady little eyes. There were probably decades of stale potato chip crumbs in the deep recesses of the recliner, and they'd find every last speck.

But this room was also devoid of people.

Two doorways, both with doors hanging by a single hinge, revealed a bedroom and bathroom. They were both filthy, but empty.

He'd have to check upstairs.

As he placed his foot on the first step, it let out a groan like his old man used to do, trying to take a shit. The next step was more like the squeak of his old lady when she got pissed about his drinkin'.

Oh hell, he thought. *Just get it over with.*

He stomped up the stairs, rattling the boards as he went. At the top, he swung the light around, quickly covering the expanse of the entire second floor.

These old houses had tiny attic rooms, usually open without even a closet. It was in a room like this that he'd grown up, along with four siblings.

But this attic room was empty.

He shined the light on the rotted old mattress in one corner. *Plenty of evidence that thing's gettin' regular use, though.* He shook his head with a shiver. *Why'd JP want to meet tonight, anyway?*

4

He wasn't in the mood for this shit.

He went back down the stairs and cautiously sat down on the wooden dining room chair, lest it collapse under him.

Taking a pack of cigarettes from his jacket pocket, he shook one out, grabbed it with his lips, then stuffed the pack back in his pocket.

Next, he pulled out a lighter, struck it five times before it lit, then took a long drag before easing back in the chair and dropping the lighter on the table.

"Now we wait," he said to no one, his accent only slightly Cajun.

This was his MO. Never walk into a situation that you haven't fully analyzed. You don't want no surprises. Once, he'd seen a rat cause all kinds of hell when some jack with the jitters, toying with his own pistol, had accidentally fingered the trigger and shot his nuts off.

Nope. None of that shit. I'm one cool muthafuckin' cat.

Not that he had anything to worry about on this particular night. He'd met with JP plenty of times and knew the man would be late, like always. He'd bum a cigarette first thing, like always. They'd shoot the shit about nothing for, like, ten minutes, just like always, and then they'd talk money and JP'd be on his way.

It was always a different place, but always predictable.

There was a scraping noise from the kitchen. He swung the beam of his flashlight around. The rat eyed him from the corner, its nose scrunched up, sniffing the air.

"*Je* be gone outta hyere real soon, *ami*," the man said, slipping into full Cajun, since he was sure that was all the rat understood.

The rat froze, staring, then seemed to shrug.

"Whatever, *bougre*."

He took another long draw on the cigarette.

5

He could've been a plumber, like his old man, and worked regular hours, spending his evenings at home with the old lady, listening to her bitch and moan all the time about making ends meet. Or maybe get a gig like his brother, working at the downtown hotel, all high and mighty, wearing a fancy suit and tie for a uniform, kissing ass all day, calling everybody "sir" and "ma'am," then still spend his evenings at home with his old lady, listening to her bitch and moan about something else.

No, he thought. *I'm my own man. None of that shit. Got my own business and doin' just fine. I come and go when I damned well please and don't tell nobody 'bout it. Wasn't nobody's damn business anyway.*

Sure, he had a boss. But that was different. As long as he produced, he never got any shit. And he produced. He had the whole district. The key was keeping others off his turf.

Over the years, he'd found a surefire way to do that. Anyone in Saint Roch who even thought about selling would get a visit from him, where he would calmly and clearly explain the situation. This was his turf. Period.

Ha! Accept it, or you's alligator bait.

He glanced at his Audemars Piguet watch, pausing to admire how the face glowed. That's how you knew it was the real thing.

It was a quarter past one, and JP was late. Nothing new there. Yet, something wasn't sitting right with him, and he still couldn't put a finger on it.

He got up from the chair and moved to the living room again, where he looked out the broken front window to the street.

He wasn't worried about being spotted. He was deep in the shadows of the dark room.

A lone streetlight partially illuminated a small part of the block a few houses down. The rest of the neighborhood was so dark, the illuminated spot looked like a circular gateway into another dimension.

Somethin' outta one of those late-night Twilight Zone reruns.

He thought he caught a glimpse of a stray dog, skulking in the shadows along a fence down the street. Maybe not.

He sensed something odd about that light. Had it been on when he came in?

He stepped back deeper into the shadows, uneasy.

Of course it was. Get a grip, man.

He shined his red flashlight around the empty kitchen again. "Where'd you go, you dumbass rat?"

The back door blasted open, and something came flying in. It rolled across the floor, hit the cabinet with a clink, and started hissing.

"What the fuck?"

The door flung open again and a muffled voice yelled, "NOPD! This is a raid!"

"Shit!" He spun and made for the front door.

It flung open and a bright light blinded him.

"Get down on the floor!"

Then the gas hit him. His eyes burned and his nostrils seared with pain. He dropped to his knees, mucous flowing from his nose.

"Put your hands in the air! Hands in the air!"

He retched as the gas filled his lungs. "I can't... I can't breathe."

"Put your hands in the air! You're under arrest."

CHAPTER TWO

It was getting dark, and they were in a hurry. Why Jesse didn't just go with the original plan—shoot the two men and run—Charity wasn't sure. Some sense of fair play, she guessed.

Or maybe he just didn't want *any* witnesses.

Charity glanced back at the handful of people sitting at three tables behind the restaurant they'd just left. The outdoor dining area consisted of no more than eight small tables scattered around the sand under a wood-framed, metal-roofed awning. There was a small stage and, like most of the tables, it was also empty.

None of the patrons gave her and the three men any notice.

All she'd had to do was show a little cleavage and firm belly by tying her shirttail under her breasts and the two men had become slathering Neanderthals, so intent on watching her every move that they never noticed her partner slip up behind them.

Jesse had said these two men could be the most dangerous adversaries they'd ever encountered. But that hadn't yet proven to be true.

"Keep walking straight to the water," Jesse ordered the two men, as they passed between clusters of palms. "Turn right just below the high tide washup."

The tide was low now, and the line of floating debris and foam left by the previous high was visible in the moonlight.

"Turn right," Jesse ordered, as they reached the tide line. "And keep walking."

Charity glanced over at her partner, striding confidently beside her, both of them holding handguns trained on the backs of the two men.

Jesse McDermitt was incredibly tall. At five-nine, Charity was at eye level with most men. He wasn't a giant or anything, but well over six feet in height, with broad shoulders, a narrow waist, and powerful arms and legs. He had the kind of rugged good looks that never seemed to age.

In near total darkness, away from the lights of the bar and not quite close enough to those of the resort spilling out onto the sand ahead, Jesse ordered the two men to pick up their pace, but not too fast.

She and Jesse had left their dive gear just a few hundred yards down the beach. What he planned to do when they got there, she had no idea.

They'd used rebreathers to get to shore from Jesse's boat, *Gaspar's Revenge*, and the rigs only had a single regulator attached to a full-face mask. They couldn't swim the murderer and his accomplice back out to the boat under the cover of the sea.

Not alive anyway.

Dead and underwater? Why remove the bodies? It was already decided that this was a clean-up mission and these two men's fates were sealed.

Nobody knew she and Jesse were there. It was the way Charity worked, and under Jesse's tutelage, she'd gotten better at it.

"What is it you think I did?" the taller of the two men asked, turning his head slightly.

"Shut up and keep moving," Charity ordered.

His name was Anthony Paladin, a former Marine Corps spec-ops guy gone bad. He knew Jesse somehow. They were both Marines, but Charity doubted they'd served together. Jesse had retired from the military more than twenty years ago, and Paladin was probably just a kid then. But they knew each other.

Maybe that was why she and Jesse didn't just put a bullet in both men's brains and leave.

The smaller man, Cordova, turned to Paladin. "You gonna take that shit off this split-tail, man?"

"Watch your mouth," Jesse snarled. "She's killed better operatives than either of you for saying far less, *and* with her bare hands."

Charity's eyes cut to her right for an instant. Why had he told them that? Much of what she'd done for Homeland Security was still classified, and everything she'd done for the CIA was completely covert—need to know—and neither of these men needed to know *anything* about her.

Paladin looked back over his shoulder at Charity, then shifted his eyes to Jesse for an instant. "Is she the whacked bitch Stockwell told me about? The one who fed a bunch of panty-waisted Nazis to a school of piranha?"

He knows Jesse and *Colonel Stockwell*, she thought. And apparently, Paladin knew a little about her, as well.

"Shut up and keep—"

"Hey!" a voice shouted from behind them, distracting Jesse. It was a woman. "Hey, Mistuh! Yuh got to pay for yuh drinks!"

In her peripheral vision, Charity caught two almost simultaneous movements as time seemed to slow, and her senses went into overdrive at the woman's shout.

Jesse looked back, and Paladin spun to attack.

She shifted her aim toward the threat, but just as her finger was tightening on the trigger, the smaller man moved with cat-like reflexes, spinning toward her.

She started to bring her pistol back to the aggressor in front of her, trying to will her body to react faster.

But suddenly there was a gunshot.

The woman who'd yelled behind them—most likely the waitress at the bar—screamed like she'd seen a monster rise up out of the water.

A small wave crested on the shore to her left as the echo of the shot faded.

Cordova's shoulder collided with the barrel of Charity's gun, jamming it so hard into her palm, she felt it all the way to her elbow, numbing her arm and causing her to lose her grip as the two of them went down onto the sand.

It was a lucky impact. Another microsecond and she'd have pressed the trigger and ended Cordova's pathetic life, then turned and done the same with Paladin.

What they should have done at the restaurant.

She landed on her back with Cordova on top of her, driving his shoulder into her midsection. She couldn't contain the air in her lungs as his weight drove into her and she grunted in pain.

Raising her legs high, she locked them around Cordova's body, just below his armpits.

Then she began to squeeze.

Charity allowed Cordova to pin her hands on either side of her head.

He leaned in close, and she could smell the cheap vodka on his breath as an ugly, lecherous smile crossed his face. With her long legs wrapped around him, he began thrusting his hips against her.

"Feelin' a little wild, are ya?" Cordova growled into her ear as he continued his lewd act.

"Old man's still got some fire," she heard Paladin growl. "Too bad your girlfriend don't."

She ignored the taunt, aimed to distract Jesse, and hoped he did too.

Cordova leaned closer, keeping her hands pinned helplessly over her head, right where she wanted him.

He laughed lustily, biting at her shoulder as he continued to slam his pelvis between her legs.

Let him get his jollies off, she thought, as she lay docilely beneath him, keeping a tight rein on her inner demons.

Time is on our side, she implored them. *Be patient.*

He didn't know what trouble he was in yet, but he would soon realize it.

When Cordova released one of her hands and pawed at her open blouse, trying to untie the knot at her sternum, she lashed out and caught him flush on the jaw with a left fist.

He again pinned her hand, shook his head, then leaned in once more. "Ya like it rough, huh..." He huffed, getting just a little air into his lungs. "This is gonna be... a whole lotta fu—"

Charity squeezed harder, forcing the air out of him before he could finish the sentence and try to draw another breath.

"AARRGGHH!" he croaked, expelling what precious little air he had left.

Charity pressed her heels into Cordova's back, driving her pelvis into his diaphragm while her thighs continued their merciless squeeze from the sides.

Cordova suddenly became aware that maybe he wasn't the

aggressor so much as her prey. He began pushing at her legs, wrapped around his torso, but her thighs were too high for him to get any force against them with his hands.

With a combined leg length of eighty inches and her ankles locked at his lower back, she had far more leverage than he.

He tried to push down on her hips, to force the leg lock lower, so he could breathe.

But Charity only redoubled her effort, putting her entire body into the exertion.

Cordova tried to hammer her belly with his fist, but he was already fading, and her core was tight, so the blow had no effect.

From a young age, Charity had had long legs and an equally long torso. By developing them to be stronger every year, she'd used her dolphin kick to propel her quite literally onto the U.S. Olympic Swim Team, where she'd won a bronze medal at the Sydney games in 2000. She was only twenty then, still in college, and looking forward to the next four years of competition and training as she finished her degree and went on to post-graduate studies.

Then the attacks on 9/11 had happened and her swimming career had ended.

If anything, her legs were even stronger at forty-three than they had been when she was an Olympian.

She could see the panic in Cordova's eyes as realization set in.

She waited for another opening.

He raised himself to his knees, lifting her hips up and pushing down as hard as he could against the same flat belly that had caught his attention minutes earlier.

With only her head and shoulders on the sand, back arched to maintain the leg lock, she was able to apply even greater force, hearing and feeling the satisfying sound of one of his ribs breaking in her snake-like embrace.

When he arched his back for maximum leverage, tilting his head back in one last supreme effort, Charity struck.

Executing a quick sit-up and using his body to support them both, her body whipped upward, and her right hand lashed out in a single punch to the throat.

In kung fu, it was called a leopard blow, or *hiraken*: only the last two knuckles of the fingers curled, with the thumb alongside the forefinger and the rigid third knuckle. It made the fist look like a flattened leopard's paw.

Cordova gagged and began to convulse as he fell forward. His hands moved instantly to his crushed larynx.

Charity twisted her body so he landed beside her, with her legs still wrapped around his torso, wincing as his weight came down on the inside of her thigh, but not letting up on the squeeze.

She grabbed him around the head with both arms, pulling his face viciously to her chest in a deadly embrace—the top of his spinal column in her arms and the bottom between her legs.

Bending her face close to his ear and wrapping her arms around his head, which she held tightly between her breasts, she used the muscles of her trunk to twist and pull his body as she wrenched his head from side to side against her chest.

"You like this, you fucking perv?" she hissed quietly, steadily gyrating her pelvis, squirming like a python, and twisting his body in an unnatural way as she held his head tightly.

Her movements became frenzied and maniacal as she sensed him slipping away. She thrust down hard with her legs while jerking his head one way, then the other.

He was oxygen-deprived and helpless, drooling on her chest as she continued her deadly twisting, jerking, and pulling with her whole body.

Then there was an audible snap, and Cordova's body went limp.

She rolled him away, moving close and looking into his vacant eyes.

"Was it good for you, asshole?" she sneered, then spat on him and pushed him away to extricate her left leg from beneath him.

She rose, feet planted wide in the sand, as she looked down at Cordova's inert body.

His head lay almost sideways on his shoulder, the skull no longer connected to the fragile vertebrae of the spine. His blank eyes looked up lifelessly at the moon and stars.

"You okay?" she heard from behind her.

Charity wheeled around, staying low and bringing her hands up as her wet hair whipped across her face.

Jesse was standing over Paladin, who was writhing in the sand, also clutching at his throat.

She calmed and stood erect, letting her hands fall to her sides as she moved closer.

Paladin was barely struggling, and looked to be slowly strangling himself, his hands clutching at his throat.

"What do we do about him?" Charity asked.

Jesse glanced down at the man who Charity was sure he'd once known.

"He's dead," he replied flatly. "Let's get out of here."

She looked over at Jesse, one of few men she'd ever fully trusted, her gaze traveling from his face to his broad chest, down across his navel. Her breathing was labored, and his chest heaved from the exertion and excitement, as well.

She'd always been attracted to Jesse, and had several times come very close to following through with that raw, physical urge she felt in his presence, that same primal urge she was feeling right then. She wanted nothing more than to grab him and wrestle him to the sand in a fervent embrace.

She took a step toward him as he started to turn, moving to get away from the scene. But she grabbed his arm and spun him toward her, locking one leg around his and nearly climbing him to get that first kiss, then another, her hunger growing.

They fell onto the sand, intertwined in one another's arms, pulling insistently at each other's clothing as she kissed him with more passion and emotion than she'd felt for any man.

CHAPTER THREE

July 1, 2023
Bay of Campeche

Charity woke suddenly, covered in a light sweat, as she sat up in bed with nothing but a thin sheet tangled around her legs and partially covering her. It slipped down to her waist, exposing her skin to the cool night air coming through the overhead hatch.

For a moment, she didn't know where she was.

The air on her skin tingled and heightened her senses.

She'd had strange dreams before—some weird, some erotic—and she'd had the occasional nightmare about the men she'd lost or those she'd killed since then, as well as the recurring images of her ordeal in Afghanistan. These visions often played back in her subconscious mind with frightening realism.

But this one had seemed more vivid and real than any she'd ever had.

At least, right up until the end.

She blinked, recalling the day she'd last seen Jesse. "That's never happened before."

The double assassination had occurred—that part of the dream was real. It had happened four months earlier, in a cove in Marsh

Harbor on the Bahamian island of Great Abaco.

But she and Jesse had immediately dashed down the beach, gathered their dive gear, and then swum back out to his boat, barely escaping a police search less than twenty minutes later.

It *hadn't* ended with them making love on the wet sand, waves washing over them like in some sappy movie from the 1950s.

Her breathing was as labored as it had been that night on the beach. She stared vacantly through the open door into her boat's salon and galley. "What is wrong with me?" she said aloud.

The upper hatch over the companionway was closed and locked, but the small batwing doors below it were open. The cool summer breeze coming through the hatch in her little V-berth drifted back through the boat and out the companionway hatch, keeping the interior cooler.

Charity shivered again, though the temperature was probably still in the eighties.

She picked up her watch from the small shelf by her knee. It was almost five o'clock. The sun would be up in a little over an hour.

Pushing thoughts of the dream from her mind, Charity rose from her bed and went into the galley to start the coffeemaker and make breakfast—the same routine she did every morning aboard *Wind Dancer.*

Being so far from shore and completely alone, there was no need to get dressed, but she did pull her apron over her head, cinching the ties at her back, to avoid getting anything hot on her skin.

When she'd anchored the previous night, there had been no other boats in sight, and she doubted that had changed. It was the middle of summer and most cruisers had moved back up north to cooler climes.

Wind Dancer, Charity's forty-five-foot John Alden-designed cutter, had a security system that belied her antique heritage. It included motion sensors and radar alarms. If anything had come close during the night, Charity would have been alerted.

If someone were to swim out and gain access to the deck, they'd be picked up by motion sensors, then bright spreader lights would come on and an alarm would blare.

So there was no need for her to even look through the oval portholes to know there were no boats within a quarter of a mile. But she did, anyway, seeing nothing but stars reflecting on the water.

As she prepared breakfast, Charity let her mind drift back to the events of the evening when she and Jesse had caught up with Anthony Paladin.

They'd chased the man from Florida all the way up to the Northern Bahamas and had rescued three women and a man whom Paladin had kidnapped. She and Jesse had finally caught up to him and his cohort, Leonard Cordova, late at night on Great Abaco, and had then gotten the drop on them in an outdoor restaurant.

They'd been returning to where she and Jesse had left their dive gear when Paladin had attacked, taking advantage of Jesse's momentary distraction by a waitress shouting at them.

Paladin's move had forced her and Jesse to retaliate and they'd eliminated both men in a kill-or-be-killed struggle.

In Charity's opinion, the two men had gotten off easy.

When she and Jesse had returned to the Florida Keys the next evening, they'd found that Jesse's wife, who had been logistically supporting their operation, had disappeared.

Savannah McDermitt was one of only a small number of female friends Charity had, and she felt she was at least partly to blame for what had happened.

The police had been questioning Jesse in the back of his boat after the killings on the beach, and he'd needed a distraction and reinforcement of the lies he was telling them.

Knowing that Savannah was monitoring the situation using the super high- definition camera on one of Armstrong Research's satellites, Charity had been forced to use the only distraction she had at her disposal—immodestly exposing herself to the policemen, *and Jesse.*

The ruse had worked, and the cops had left almost immediately.

She'd always tried to remain professional in Jesse's presence whenever others were around, but if Savannah turned her back, Charity sometimes couldn't help teasing him.

She shook her head as she turned the omelet in the skillet. *Why do I keep doing that?*

Jesse thought it was all just her having fun at his expense, and it had been, for the most part. But for several years before he and Savannah were married, all it would have taken on Jesse's part was a simple nod of his head.

It wasn't the first time she'd used her looks as a distraction. The police had been preparing to board and search. If they'd found her and Jesse's wet dive gear in the fish box under his feet, they might have put two and two together.

So, when she'd heard Jesse tell the police that he wasn't alone, that his new bride was inside—a cover story she herself had suggested—Charity stepped out of the cabin wearing nothing but her panties and holding Savannah's bathrobe.

Though the satellite's camera couldn't pick up what they were saying, Charity had no doubt that Savannah had seen everything.

Had it been anyone else in the world, Charity wouldn't have given it a second thought. But she'd known she'd crossed a line when she did it and had then set out to find Savannah and try to explain to her that what she'd done didn't mean anything; Jesse was absolutely devoted to her.

But could she say that convincingly?

She'd met Savannah and her daughter, Flo, when they'd been in Biscayne Bay, preparing to cross over to the Bahamas, and Charity's had been the only other boat at the anchorage. The girl had only been about nine or ten at the time and Jesse didn't even know Flo was his daughter.

But Charity soon learned that he and Savannah had known one another from years before, and she'd seen the resemblance right away but never said anything about it to either of them.

More recently, Charity had attended Flo's wedding, and during the years between those events, Charity and Savannah had become friends, running into one another from time to time.

Unfortunately, they also shared a violent history.

During one of those random meetings, this one on Hoffman's Cay, several men had accosted her and Savannah while Flo was jumping into the inland blue hole located there.

Savannah's dog had killed one man, taking him over the cliff and onto the rocks below. Savannah had knocked another man out with a kick to the head, and Charity had taken care of the other two.

Then she'd sent Savannah and Flo away and dispatched the men's bodies to the bottom of the blue hole—a feast for the crabs a thousand feet down.

Some time after that, they'd run into each other again, and Charity had been able to help a very distraught Savannah in rescuing Flo, who'd been kidnapped by Savannah's ex-husband. The man had wrongly assumed Flo was *his* daughter and had wanted to use her as leverage against Savannah, who was worth millions.

He'd developed a fondness for drugs and cheap island girls, which later led to his death at Jesse's hands.

To say she and the couple were intertwined would be an understatement. Charity had become very fond of Flo, even mentoring her in swimming. So it was natural for her to have become a bit unraveled herself while trying to find the girl. She'd let slip a few things that it probably would have been better Savannah didn't know.

Charity had recognized the young girl's swimming ability and had helped her hone her natural talent over the years until Flo was ready. Then, she'd introduced the young woman to her old coach, who'd been a scout for the U.S. Olympic Swim Team at the time.

The University of Florida had offered Flo a full-ride athletic scholarship, which she'd turned down, allowing another girl to accept in her place since Jesse had already paid for her college several years before, and she'd already decided on the UF swim team anyway.

Charity's nostalgic smile disappeared when she remembered why she was tracking Savannah. She steeled herself for a face-to-face apology she hoped her friend would accept as she finished her breakfast, washing the omelet down with strong Costa Rican coffee.

It'd been seventeen weeks since she'd flown away from Jesse and Savannah's island. The man had been a wreck, wallowing in self-loathing, and though he didn't come right out and say it, she knew he at least partially blamed her.

In the darkness, Charity washed the one dish, one fork, one knife, and one pan, then dried them and put them away.

It was part of her morning ritual, and the menu varied only

slightly as to what went into her omelet.

She didn't need the lights on to move around inside her boat; she knew where everything was—every beam, each cabinet or drawer handle, and most importantly, the accesses to the several weapons hidden around the boat.

She headed to the companionway, turned off the alarm, and unlocked the overhead hatch.

Cautiously, she slid it open and stepped up one step so only her eyes were above the hatch. Then she slowly scanned the water all around her boat. Not a ripple.

Alarms and sensors were great, but a visual check was better. Charity had been surprised more than once by middle-of-the-night intruders.

Most had been relatively harmless but overly amorous men she'd met who thought it okay to peek through windows. They'd learned a valuable life lesson for their transgression.

Twice it had been men sent to kill her.

Those men didn't get any *life* lessons.

CHAPTER FOUR

For quite a few years, Charity Styles had lived almost completely off the grid. She'd been nearly invisible, consciously choosing to shun human interaction unless absolutely necessary.

She'd made a lot of enemies over the years, some of them wielding great power, some simply irate wives, who could be equally dangerous at times.

She knew there was a price on her head in more than one country. She also knew that in most cases, the wanted poster for her showed only a blank picture. In parts of Venezuela and Mexico, she was called *El Gata*. In some Middle Eastern countries, she was known simply as *Qatil*—Assassin.

Few ever saw her, and fewer still would remember, as she took great pains to change her appearance and blend in with others whenever possible.

Charity spent a full two minutes slowly turning on the companionway steps, looking for anything out of the ordinary as she enjoyed the fresh air and another cup of coffee.

The small cove she was anchored in, a mile from shore, was still deserted—not a boat in sight. The cove was in the Bay of Campeche near the small town of Seybaplaya on the west side of the Yucatan Peninsula.

To the east, she could just make out the white sand beach in the low light of predawn. Above it, the tops of swaying palm trees were silhouetted against the graying sky.

She stared forlornly at the shoreline, thinking back to that other beach on Great Abaco.

She'd left Jesse the morning after they'd returned from the Bahamas, intent on finding Savannah. That had been nearly four months ago.

Savannah had gotten only one day's head start in her slow-moving trawler, and Charity had thought she could find her quickly using her helicopter. Those who'd seen Savannah leave the Rusty Anchor early the previous morning had all said she was headed steadily south.

But Charity had known that Savannah's course was meant to throw Jesse's friend, Rusty Thurman, off. She'd left just after sunrise and Rusty was known to be an early riser, so Savannah would have realized he'd seen her leave.

She'd also been spotted ten miles south of the Keys, still heading due south toward Cuba, a hundred miles away.

Certain that the island nation wasn't Savannah's destination, Charity had flown her helo away from Jesse's island at dawn—almost twenty-four hours after Savannah had left—and followed the chain of islands toward the mainland.

There was a reason Savannah had left at dawn. As a cruiser herself, Charity knew that an early departure usually meant a long crossing.

So, she felt sure Savannah hadn't just gone south to throw anyone off, then turned around and disappeared into one of the hundreds of marinas located in the Keys.

Instead, she'd concentrated her initial search to the Intracoastal

Waterway and the edge of the Gulf Stream.

She'd followed the Keys up to the mainland, where she'd refueled in Miami and began hopping around the islands, cays, and quiet coves of South Florida and the nearby Bahamian islands.

In one day, at full speed, and not stopping for anything, Charity had estimated that Savannah's boat could probably cover more than two hundred nautical miles. It was possible that she could have made it to the Bahamas on that first day, easily. It would be the logical place to disappear, with hundreds of islands at her disposal.

Or if she'd gone the other way, she could have made it almost to the western end of Cuba with no place to stop or hide until she got to Mexico, Texas, or one of the Gulf Coast states. Less likely, with a kid in tow.

Having a young boy with her, Charity doubted Savannah would take *Sea Biscuit* that far and would have gone east, likely anchoring for the night somewhere in the Upper Keys or Biscayne Bay. Or even gone as far as the nearer Bahama islands.

Charity had refueled again that first day in Nassau and had then continued searching around Andros Island and up to Bimini, then headed south, thinking Savannah might not have stopped for the night.

She'd finally refueled late in the afternoon in Jamaica, knowing it was futile to continue when it had been thirty-six hours since Savannah had left.

By then, Charity had realized that Savannah could just as easily have turned west instead of east. That, or her boat was faster than Charity thought.

She'd also come to the conclusion that searching by air at that point would take forever, given the day-and-a-half lead Savannah had by then.

With darkness approaching, Charity had flown back to Grand Cayman with a new plan, knowing that the only way to find Savannah would be by boat, and by her wits.

When she'd arrived back in Grand, she'd called Flo, knowing if Savannah had told anyone where she was going, it would be her daughter.

Savannah *had* called her; Flo had at least told her that much. She'd said that Savannah was okay but didn't give her a reason for going off like she had, only that she needed to get away for a while.

Flo had promised her mother she wouldn't tell anyone about anything else they'd discussed. And Charity knew it was hopeless to press the point.

Flo hadn't seemed angry with her, so Charity doubted if Savannah had told her daughter what had happened.

Wind Dancer was always provisioned and ready, so, after a good night's sleep, Charity had set sail for the Yucatan Peninsula of Mexico.

She figured the best way to find Savannah would be to listen to the cruiser nets, which broadcast at specific times every day to keep cruisers up to speed with what was going on anywhere they might have friends or an interest.

Net was short for network, a single sideband, or SSB, broadcast from ham radio operators who were cruisers and meant for other cruisers around the world.

These daily amateur radio broadcasters almost always talked about new arrivals and departures in the clusters of places cruisers frequented. They also gave local tide and weather updates, provided information about things like ride sharing to airports, local events coming up, and even gave businesses a chance to tell cruisers in the area what they had going on.

Over the years, Charity had compiled a list of almost a hundred cruiser nets all over the Caribbean, along with their broadcast times and frequencies. Sometimes, the person who made the announcements would change, but the time and frequency were always the same.

On the third day out of Grand, she was listening to a net near Cancun, when the woman broadcasting had mentioned that a boat named *Sea Biscuit* had arrived late the previous day and departed that morning, but she didn't mention where the boat was headed or even the direction.

It could be a different boat entirely, but it was the only clue she'd had.

The morning of her fourth day out, as Charity had neared the Yucatan, she'd been faced with a decision—bear off to the east and head toward Central and South America, or west and follow the Mexican coastline toward Texas.

She'd chosen east, for no other reason than she assumed that if someone was hell-bent on getting away and not being found, they wouldn't restrict themselves to the Gulf of Mexico.

But as the days and weeks passed, Charity began to feel it was a hopeless cause. Savannah was off the grid, on a boat that was designed for long-range exploration. She could be anywhere.

Charity knew just how easy it was for a person to vanish on a boat. Out on the open sea, line of sight, and therefore, normal VHF marine radio and radar range, extended only about four miles in any direction, a little more for the radio and radar, since they were mounted higher. Beyond that, anything that was out there would be over the horizon and invisible, basically giving a person on a boat a view of about fifty square miles of water to look at. While it sounded like a large area, Charity knew there were at least twenty thousand locations, just in the Caribbean Basin alone, where, if a boat were at each one, none could see another.

Then there were the thousands of islands, coves, inlets, harbors, anchorages, and marinas. It had been like looking for a needle in a field full of haystacks.

The weeks had turned into months, but Charity hadn't given up.

Then one day, Jesse had called her. They'd talked awkwardly for a few minutes before he'd told her about a note that Savannah had left, telling him not to come looking for her, that she'd be in touch when she was ready.

Charity had thought it had sounded somewhat vague, not at all like what a jealous woman would write. But what did she know?

Savannah was always one who held her cards close to her chest. And she knew how to manage Jesse, *if* such a thing could be done.

Charity had doubted Savannah would go all the way to South America, so thought that she would have probably stopped somewhere along the eastern coast, or the island of Cozumel.

She found lots of cruisers along the way. Some were American or Canadian expats. Most were harmless. A couple weren't.

If you poked around in small coves and marinas long enough, you eventually drew the attention of the lowlifes. At least, that had been Charity's experience.

Finally, during the third week, she'd reached Cozumel, where she decided to hole up and wait, resting, reprovisioning, and listening to the nets.

She listened and listened some more. For weeks, she'd tuned into every net she had a record of, waiting to hear any mention of her friend.

She also conducted extensive internet searches, using her own private satellite account, which nobody else knew about.

In early May, Charity's patience had finally paid off. She'd been changing anchorages every few days, so as to not draw attention, just moving back and forth between the island of Cozumel and Cancún on the mainland. During one such relocation, she'd heard Savannah's boat's name mentioned again.

It was a guy broadcasting from a small marina near Progreso, on the northwest side of the Yucatan.

Charity had immediately turned north, set sail, and killed the engine.

Though it was over three hundred nautical miles, *Wind Dancer* had gotten her to Progreso late the following night, just forty hours after hearing Savannah had been there.

While her friend might have been hampered with caring for a young boy and doing all the navigating and piloting herself, Charity wasn't.

Wind Dancer was fully automated and could sail herself around the clock for days on end. Charity usually napped on the bench next to the helm during solo night passages, waking every hour to make sure everything was okay.

In one hour, her boat could move more than five nautical miles, and the radar alert was set for eight. So, checking every hour usually only amounted to opening one eye and looking at the sky ahead.

Calculating when Savannah had departed Progreso and she'd left Cozumel, Charity knew when to start looking at every boat and anchorage she passed a lot more closely.

So, when Charity had arrived near Progreso, she was certain that Savannah hadn't passed her and had likely gone around the west side of the Yucatan toward the Bay of Campeche.

There were very few coves to anchor in, or marinas to rent a slip from. But being on the west side of the peninsula, shielded from the prevailing easterly wind by the giant land mass, the near shore waters were protected most of the time and boaters just anchored off the beach in whatever water depth they needed. Even ten or fifteen miles out, where the wind was better, the sea state was almost always calm.

Though it was dark when *Wind Dancer* approached the pier and anchorage at Progreso, Charity could clearly see every boat anchored or tied to the pier. Savannah's wasn't among them, and she was sure she hadn't passed her along the way.

Nor was a certain fishing boat tied up at the dock. Years ago, she'd met a handsome young fisherman there.

Not finding Savannah in Progreso, she'd started searching slowly along the Yucatan's west coast for several more weeks, anchoring well offshore every night, stopping to reprovision when needed, but always within sight of the water, and listening, always listening.

On that particular morning after breakfast and a hot shower, Charity lay in her hammock below the boom, listening to the Campeche cruiser's net, which wasn't very far from her location off Seybalaya.

The man talking had an obvious accent, which Charity guessed to be from one of the Nordic countries—Sweden or Norway, maybe.

"A shooting occurred yesterday," he said, as if reading each word carefully. "It involved the... rundown-looking trawler that has been spotted in the bay these last few weeks. The trawler was attacked by who are thought to be foot-soldiers of the... *Cártel del Pacífico Sur*, operating a small, inflatable boat."

Charity sat up in the hammock and propped herself on her elbows, listening intently. Kidnappings and violence were almost commonplace in many parts of Central and South America, but she hadn't heard about many taking place in the remote areas of the Yucatan.

"The trawler... shot back..." the broadcaster continued, in halting English, "...reportedly killing one of the pirates and... driving their boat away."

Shooting accurately from a moving boat took a skilled marksman, and this piqued Charity's curiosity, along with the fact that it was a trawler. Not that there was a lack of trawlers in these waters, but these two factors together made the occurrence unusual... and familiar.

Charity swung her feet to the cabin's rooftop and listened as the man described the boat as an older Taiwanese trawler, with rubber tire fenders and rust stains spilling from her scuppers. He reported that after the small boat broke off, the trawler fled to the north. Then he went on to say that it was believed that the trawler belonged to a cartel that was a rival of the attackers.

Charity didn't think the trawler he was talking about was *Sea Biscuit*. Savannah was a capable woman and being married to a man who was once one of the Marine Corps' top marksmen, Charity had no doubt that Savannah *could* have driven attackers away, but the description of the boat didn't jibe with Savannah's at all. She'd never let her boat get into such a state. And in just four months, *Sea Biscuit* couldn't have become that badly out of shape, even if Savannah tried.

Then the broadcaster had removed all doubt in Savannah's mind when he mentioned the departure of *Sea Biscuit* early that morning.

Charity moved closer to the helm's speaker.

"It was great having... *Sea Biscuit* and her crew with us... this past week," the broadcaster said. "We hope to... run into you again, one day."

He didn't say which way *Sea Biscuit* had headed, but it didn't matter. If she'd gone south, Charity would have seen her, or would very soon. Campeche was only twenty or so miles up the coast, three hours or so for *Sea Biscuit.*

Feelings of excitement and dread came over Charity at the same time. Savannah was close. She might finally find her. But she'd have to face her. There was no other way. She'd have to admit her feelings and apologize.

There was no way around it. It had to be done. Resolved, she went below to get dressed and get ready to head north, toward Campeche.

While she'd been on deck, she'd felt the wind on her face coming over the massive peninsula to the east. She'd have a strong beam reach and calm seas. With both headsails deployed along with the main, *Wind Dancer* could do almost nine knots under these conditions. She could be in Campeche in a little over two hours, and Savannah had left there just a couple of hours earlier.

It was the closest she'd been to finding her friend in four months.

CHAPTER FIVE

Twenty minutes after hearing the broadcast from Campeche, *Wind Dancer* sailed off anchor and turned north with her mainsail and genoa deployed. The wind was high enough she could make the run with just the main and genny, without having to take a reef to reduce sail area.

Charity added a waypoint on the plotter, a mile off the coast of Campeche, then set the autopilot so she could zoom in and study the rhumb line that would be her course. She was looking for any shoals or other obstructions but found none. *Dancer* would have at least fourteen feet of water below her keel the whole way.

For the most part, the waters to the west of the Yucatan were shallow for quite a few miles, sloping gently from shore to sixty feet before dropping off to deep water many miles from the coast. Staying at least a mile offshore, where the depth was consistent at twenty to twenty-two feet, there would be no danger of running aground.

So, she sat back on the high, windward bench seat next to the helm and stretched her legs out, crossing them at the ankle.

The electric winch for the main sheet clicked twice behind her as the computer made a minute adjustment to the sail trim for maximum speed in a straight line.

The true wind speed was fairly constant at eighteen to nineteen knots and *Dancer* was sailing a beam reach, her fastest and most comfortable point of sail.

If the wind direction changed, the computer would trim the sails more, to maintain heading. But there was no change in the forecast and Charity had been in the area long enough to be amazed at the consistency.

The computer would also start the small generator if the autopilot's and winches' drains on the batteries became too great. That didn't happen often, though. *Dancer* had solar panels, a wind generator, even a hydro generator that produced electricity from the spinning propeller while under sail. It would take half a day before the generator would start and run for about thirty minutes to top up the batteries.

The wind and an occasional light mist from the bow felt good on Charity's face and, though the day might bring some trepidation later, she smiled.

The broadcaster had said that *Sea Biscuit* had left just after dawn, which was about two hours earlier. If Savannah headed north at her six-knot cruising speed, she'd have covered twelve nautical miles by the time Charity got underway.

She leaned over and checked *Wind Dancer's* speed on the plotter—a little over eight knots, speed over ground.

If they were both headed north, starting thirty-two miles apart, and neither stopped nor slowed, *Wind Dancer's* two-knot SOG advantage meant that she would catch *Sea Biscuit* in about sixteen hours.

The big Grand Banks was *able* to go faster, but at its top speed it would only be by a knot or two if Charity had good wind, and she did.

Fuel was Savannah's biggest problem. At full speed, *Sea Biscuit's* big diesels chugged it by the barrel. *Wind Dancer* was making eight knots using only the power of the wind.

The two solar panels on the cabin top, plus the wind and hydro generators, could keep all her batteries fully charged while underway if she didn't use the autopilot very much.

Normally, she'd sail manually for a while, then let the autopilot take over for short periods while she tended to other things. But right now, Charity needed to pay attention to any passing vessels. She was in the zone where Savannah might be if she'd headed south, instead of north. Two hours after departing would put *Sea Biscuit* only eight nautical miles ahead and closing at a combined speed of fourteen knots. They could be within half an hour of each other if Savannah had headed south.

Charity thought about what she'd say when she finally did catch up to Savannah. It'd been four months since they'd talked, and so far as Charity knew, Savannah hadn't contacted Jesse in all that time.

Don't come looking for me, she'd written in the letter she'd left him.

When he'd finally stumbled up the steps to his house that night, he'd appeared totally shattered—a hollow shell of a man.

It was a look Charity had never associated with McDermitt.

She imagined Jesse pining away the weeks and months, secluding himself by his phone, hair and beard unkempt, and sleeping in his clothes.

She felt responsible for all of that, and in her mind his situation had probably declined in the last four months. For all she knew, he might just as easily be dating a Key West stripper already, but she doubted anything close to that was going on.

That was the old Jesse. No, he was hurting too much now for that.

She thought about calling him to let him know she was close to finding Savannah, but she'd never told him she was looking for his wife in the first place.

The few times Charity had spoken to Flo since her initial call, she'd been told the same thing. "Mom's okay. She has to sort things out in her own way, and it sometimes takes her a while." Then she'd laugh and remind Charity that she'd lived aboard *Sea Biscuit* with her mother for most of her life and she and the boat were both very capable. She'd also told her of the many times she'd done the same thing over the years—the two of them running when someone got too close or there was trouble on the horizon. It wasn't anything Savannah would be unaccustomed to.

Flo was always polite and had never seemed worried, which troubled Charity. Her mother was alone with a ten-year-old in a slow, old boat on the open ocean.

But Flo knew her better than anyone, and didn't seem to think her leaving as she had was out of character, or that it meant the end of her parents' relationship.

But maybe she hadn't told Flo the truth. Maybe she was feeling too humiliated.

Then there was the relationship between father and daughter. Charity hadn't asked Flo if she'd talked to Jesse about what was going on, but assumed she had. And from Flo's upbeat attitude, she also assumed that Jesse hadn't told her what Charity had done.

Another relationship on the rocks because of that one stupid stunt. A sour bubble formed in Charity's stomach. She rose and went forward, checking the rigging as she'd always done right after setting sail. It was a habit; she made the check every few hours during a long crossing as well. This morning, it was an excuse to move away from her thoughts.

LIABLE CHARITY

At the bow, she paused, holding the forestay in her left hand to steady herself as she rode up and down the swells with her vessel, letting all other thoughts float away on the wind.

It was at times like this, when she was alone and out of sight of land, that Charity felt more connected to *Wind Dancer*. The two became one, and Charity could sense her boat's movements and was infinitely in tune with them.

Two hours later, having seen only two sailboats, she was nearing Campeche, and, like at most anchorages in the area, she could tell at a glance that *Sea Biscuit* wasn't there.

Knowing that Savannah had at least made contact with one person among the small number of obvious liveaboard cruisers, Charity decided to stop and get a feel for the locals. She'd gained about five miles, but if she kept her stop to just an hour, she wouldn't lose much more than she'd gained and could easily catch up after she talked to some people.

She hailed Campeche anchorage on channel sixteen—the international hailing and distress frequency—and asked if there was a harbormaster or mooring balls, though she was pretty sure there were neither.

A woman with a bit of an accent replied quickly that it was just a sandy anchorage with good hold, and that she and her husband were on the farthest boat to the south.

Over the years, Charity had found that whoever was first to offer assistance to a newly arriving cruiser was often the friendliest, and therefore, usually the most knowledgeable about what was going on locally.

And sometimes, they ran the net.

The man she'd heard had a strong Nordic accent—she'd thought he'd sounded like a Norwegian swimmer she'd dated briefly. But the

41

woman on the radio had almost no accent and Charity couldn't place the remnants of it. European, she was sure, but was it the same as the man who'd given the update?

"One way to find out," Charity said out loud, switching the autopilot to standby and turning the small wheel.

She picked the southernmost boat out of the group and palmed the wooden handles of the wheel with practiced ease, pointing upwind about as high as *Wind Dancer* could sail.

At the other end of the anchorage, and a bit farther from shore, a large, expensive-looking motor yacht, easily eighty feet, rode sedately on its anchor, its white hull and dark-tinted windows glistening in the midday sun. It had an elegant, rakish design that made it look fast just sitting there.

There were four other boats in the anchorage. Two appeared to be local fishing boats, called *pangas*. There was also a small sloop, about twenty-five feet, and a beautiful Leopard power catamaran about the same length as *Wind Dancer*–forty-four feet. But where *Dancer* had a long bowsprit forward, the catamaran was all hulls, either one of which provided more living space than her whole boat, with a large salon and galley connecting the two hulls.

The foresail luffed slightly, and Charity steered lightly away from the wind, rubbing the wheel's handle gently. "Just looking, *Miss Dancer.*"

She had once thought that a catamaran, whether power or sail, would be a safer and faster boat than a monohull, not to mention having more than double the space. But then she'd heard a guy in a tiki bar talking about the differences and something he'd said stuck with her. A catamaran was just as stable upside down as it was right side up.

A monohull, with its heavier keel far below the surface, would

42

always right itself if knocked down. It might lose its mast, sweep the decks clear, and even roll completely over, but it would *always* right itself.

She set the autopilot, then went forward along the canted side deck and removed the safety chain from the anchor.

When she got back to the helm, she disengaged the autopilot and activated the computer's line control and ground tackle systems.

As she neared a spot about a hundred feet away from and a little ahead of a beautiful Chinese junk, Charity turned *Wind Dancer* into the wind and waited as the large mainsail luffed over her head.

As the boat slowed, she activated the foresails' furlers and main halyard winch controls. All three sails began to furl as the wind stopped *Dancer's* forward momentum and started pushing her back.

Charity released the brake on the windlass and let the anchor down slowly as the sails continued to furl, all the lines being controlled by the computer.

The water was only eleven feet deep, so when the chain counter showed fifteen, she paused the windlass for a second to allow the ground tackle to straighten itself as the wind slowly pushed *Dancer* away from the coast.

Then she started paying out more rode, the chain clinking across the rollers. With the sails fully furled and the chain counter showing sixty-five feet, Charity stopped and locked the windlass, then started the "iron genny." She reversed the small diesel engine for a moment, digging the large anchor deep into the sand, then shifted to neutral again and shut off the engine.

She noticed a blond woman in a bathing suit on the junk watching her as she went forward to reconnect the safety chain to the anchor rode.

"Hello!" the woman called out from the junk. "Very neatly done!"

"Thanks!" Charity called back, recognizing the voice from the radio. "Is there much tidal swing here?"

"We've been here three months," the woman called back, "and we use the mast as a sundial now. There is a bit of a current to the north farther offshore, but almost none here, and a steady wind that rarely changes. You'll point this way the whole time you're here."

"I'm Gabby," Charity called back, using her alias. "Thanks for the information."

"Karina!" the woman called back. "Would you care to join us for lunch? My husband has just started to prepare it."

In Charity's travels, she'd found many cruisers to be standoffish, preferring to spend their time alone; Charity was usually that way herself, but for reasons that were probably a lot different. Most loners didn't have multiple bounties on their heads.

She'd also met many who were outgoing and social. Charity had often been invited over by couples shortly after arriving. It was sort of a rite of passage—the married women warning the solo female sailor which guys in the anchorage were okay and which were only interested in one thing.

Sometimes, the "okay" guys were only interested in one thing, too. And on a couple of occasions, the husbands.

Charity could pretend to be that personality as well. "Ten minutes to tidy up?" she called across the water.

"Take your time," Karina shouted back. "He will be thirty minutes, at least."

Charity smiled and waved, then turned her attention to securing her boat. A clock started ticking in her mind as soon as the anchor went down. Every hour spent here meant six nautical miles more distance. She was so close, but knew after likely passing one another twice already, that information was the priority, especially recent information.

Besides, *Wind Dancer* could gobble up those miles faster and for a longer time, so she could afford some time to see if she could learn anything.

For all Charity knew, Savannah could have gone just a short distance to a marina to pick something up, or get fuel, before going the other way, and Charity could easily miss her.

The woman seemed friendly and the man doing the Campeche net also had an accent. It would seem likely that he would be Karina's husband, and they had been there a long time. It would be worth the time it would take to investigate, and possibly find out if he knew where Savannah was headed next. Charity didn't want to risk losing her again.

There wasn't a lot to do as far as securing her boat went, and after checking the furlers and anchor, she went below for a quick shower to get the salt off her skin and to change into fresh clothes. Her bikini top and shorts probably wouldn't be appropriate for lunch.

Ten minutes later, Charity emerged back on deck in tan capri pants and a lightweight, long-sleeved, pale-blue blouse, and pulled her dinghy alongside.

There was still a lot of daylight left, so she was anxious to find out what she could and get underway again.

Once she'd placed a bottle of wine under the seat, she started the little outboard, which instantly settled into a smooth idle. Then she untied the painter and sat down and moved the tiller, turning her dinghy toward the junk-rigged schooner.

Approaching the raised stern, she saw a fanciful name board

that read, *Lange Reis.*

The boat was at least sixty feet long, not counting the long bowsprit. There were two cabin tops visible, each rising four feet or so above the expansive and flat main deck. The smaller cabin was aft the mainmast and extended almost to the stern, and the larger house was between the main and foremast.

Forward of the foremast, the deck had built-in chairs and sun pads, plus a small doghouse with opening glass hatches to allow light and air into the cabin below.

Karina came out of the forecabin wearing nearly the same style of attire Charity had chosen, but in navy and white.

"The ladder is on the other side," Karina shouted, pointing around the stern.

Charity turned the dinghy and brought it up alongside the junk's port side about midship, then stood and handed Karina the painter. She waited until the woman looped it around a cleat twice, then nodded, holding the bitter end taut.

Charity's dinghy was right next to a stout-looking stainless steel boarding ladder attached to the hull. She shut off the engine, rose and lifted her seat.

"Thank you for inviting me," she said, offering the bottle up to the woman. "It was very nice of you."

Karina took the bottle. "Please come aboard. You did not have to bring anything."

Charity climbed up to the deck, then took the line from Karina and cleated it securely, standing just as a man emerged from the cabin.

"I didn't know what you were having," Charity said to Karina, "but this is a favorite of mine."

"*Goedendag,*" the tall, fair-haired man said, displaying a broad

46

smile. "I am Harald Waalkens. Welcome aboard *Lange Reis.*" He glanced quickly across the water at *Wind Dancer.* "You are... alone?"

"For the moment," Charity warily replied, recognizing his voice from the net.

Karina handed Harald the bottle. "I apologize for my husband," she said to Charity, apparently picking up on her vibe. "He did not mean to alarm. He lives in a world of numbers and... how do you say? Not skilled socially?"

She smiled. "That's okay. I get it a lot."

"Viña Cobos?" Harald asked, looking at the bottle.

"One of the great vineyards of Argentina," Charity replied. "This is their *Bramare Marchiori* Cabernet Sauvignon—one of my favorites. I'm Gabby Fleming."

The tall Dutchman extended a hand. "Thank you... for the wine. I am happy... to meet you."

"Harald only began learning English a few years ago," Karina explained. "We are from Rotterdam. Would you like to go inside out of the heat?"

Leading the way, Harald opened the door to the forward cabin, which was only three steps down from the deck.

Charity followed Karina into the main cabin, a spacious salon with a dining table large enough for ten people over on the port side and a long leather couch and two recliners to starboard. The view was spectacular, with only the smaller house at the stern blocking it.

Amidship was a minimal lower helm, and a set of stairs disappearing into what Charity guessed would be bedrooms or maybe the kitchen.

The inside air was cool, so she assumed a generator was running somewhere, though she hadn't heard it. The windows were tinted, and the room was appointed with dark wood and leather. The aft starboard corner of the salon was walled off and had a door decorated with carved inlays depicting a Chinese garden. Probably a day head.

"Your boat is beautiful," Charity said, looking around. "What does the name mean?"

She asked only because it would be expected.

"*Lange Reis* is Dutch," Karina replied. "It means 'long journey.' We bought her in Thailand, where she had been used as a liveaboard dive boat."

"And the two of you sail alone? This is a lot of boat."

Harald nodded exuberantly. "*Ja, ja*, the junk... ah... rigging is not difficult."

His watch beeped and he looked at it, then turned to his wife. "*Ik moet terug naar de keuken.*"

Harald hurried out as Karina waved a hand to the sofa across from the dining table. "Please, sit. Harald had to go to the kitchen."

"That's in the aft cabin?" Charity asked.

"Yes, along with two crew cabins below, a small workshop, and the engine room access. It is all very small back there."

Charity looked up at the woman before they sat down, something she didn't do with many women. At five-nine, Charity was taller than most, but Karina was at least an inch or two taller and Harald quite a bit more. She imagined most boats were tight spaces for the couple.

"So tell me," Karina said. "What has brought you to Campeche?"

"Actually, I'm looking for a friend," Charity replied. "Was it your husband who did the broadcast this morning on the Campeche net?"

"Yes," she replied, beaming with pride. "It was my idea. Harald took it over when another man left to go through the Panama Canal a month ago. I write it for him, and he practices it each morning before going on the air. It is great training."

Charity put on her most sincere smile. "It certainly is. He mentioned my friend's boat during the broadcast—*Sea Biscuit*. Do you know Savannah?"

The woman studied her for a moment, then returned the smile. "Yes, we met a couple of times while they were here."

Charity clapped her hands in feigned exuberance.

"How is Alberto? I haven't seen them in ages. I bet he's grown. She must have changed phones, and I guess we've not been close enough for VHF."

"Why not use the SSB?" Karina asked.

"Oh, mine is just a receiver," Charity lied, knowing she'd ask.

She needed help in *finding* where Savannah went, not in contacting her. She had to be face-to-face when she explained what happened.

"I was twenty miles south of here this morning when I heard your husband's broadcast," Charity said, as the door opened, and Harald stepped in with a loaded food tray. "Did Savannah say where she was going from here? I'd love to see them again."

Karina slid over as her husband placed dishes on the table. "*Waar ging Sea Biscuit heen?*" she asked him.

Harald looked over at her, then glanced across the table at Charity. "*Sea Biscuit?*"

"Gabby is a friend of Savannah," Karina explained. "Where did she say they were going? Was it Progreso?"

Harald looked at Charity a moment, then nodded slowly. "*Ja*, Progreso. To see a friend at... er..." He scratched at his temple, thinking, "Marina Yucatan... no... Marina Yucalpetén."

49

CHAPTER SIX

An hour later, after a couple of glasses of wine and while Harald did the dishes, Karina gave Charity a tour of their boat. It had originally had five small forward cabins for week-long dive trips, but they'd converted the three forwardmost cabins into one large master stateroom.

Charity had subtly asked Karina more about Savannah and quickly learned all she could from the woman. Savannah had arrived eight days earlier and kept to herself for the most part, visiting stores and shops with Alberto.

She'd participated in a potluck on the beach with people from the two other liveaboard boats, where she'd met and befriended a mother and daughter vacationing on the big motor yacht at the opposite end of the anchorage. They were from New Orleans, and Savannah being from South Carolina, Charity figured they'd likely gravitated toward one another—typical in anchorages all over.

It was mid-afternoon when Charity told her hosts that she needed to get back to her boat, and as they stood on *Lange Reis's* deck, a motor launch approached.

"You must stay a moment and meet the Landrys," Karina said. "They are from America as well."

Charity didn't like meeting people, but realized that leaving as other guests were arriving would be considered rude.

The launch came alongside and a dark-haired woman in the front of the boat waved. "We didn't know you had company."

"You are welcome any time," Harald called out, then caught the line a man in a uniform threw to him.

Harald took some slack out of Charity's dinghy's line, pulling it farther forward but leaving the stern close to the ladder.

The launch captain expertly moved his boat right in behind Charity's dinghy, within easy reach of the ladder from the bow.

The two women on the launch climbed the ladder and the captain found refuge from the sun under the bimini top.

"Gabby Fleming," Karina said, "this is Suzette Landry and her daughter, Harper."

"You're in that beautiful antique sailboat that arrived a few hours ago?" the older of the two asked, her voice practically dripping with honeysuckle.

"She heard Harald's broadcast this morning," Karina replied, "and he mentioned her friend Savannah."

"Where do you know her from?" Harper asked.

"From many places, actually," Charity replied. "We first met more than a decade ago in Biscayne Bay, when she and her daughter Flo were together aboard *Sea Biscuit*."

"She told me all about her," Harper said. "She and I are close to the same age and belong to the same sorority. But different schools."

"Harper kept her son busy," Suzette said, "playing games with him several evenings so Savannah and I could visit. Such a charming woman."

She would have liked to stay longer, to see if the Landrys could give her any more information, but she already knew where Savannah was going and it was a good 150 miles, so she'd likely stop for the night about halfway. Or take it slow and break it into thirds.

She decided the best idea would be to go to bed early, get underway after midnight and get fifty miles in before dawn. She should easily be able to catch up to *Sea Biscuit* before Savannah and Alberto arrived in Progreso.

"Last time I saw Alberto," Charity said, raising a hand to her waist, palm down, "he was no bigger than this."

Harper laughed. "He's a little taller now and as smart as they come."

"You didn't play chess with him for money, did you?" Charity asked, also laughing.

"Not for money, but he beat me soundly."

"Me too," Charity lied. She'd never played the boy, but had heard others say how good he was. "Did Savannah say when she was going to arrive in Progreso or how long they planned to be there? Harald only knew that was where they were going from here."

The mother and daughter looked at one another and both shook their heads.

"No, I don't recall when or how long," Suzette replied. "However, that is where she said they were going. And she said they'd be meeting an old friend there. Someone Savannah had gone to high school with back home in South Carolina."

"Then I think I'll say goodbye," Charity said. "There's only a few hours of light left and if I get underway early, I might be able to catch up to them."

Harper gazed over at *Wind Dancer*, then looked at the yacht they were on at the other end of the anchorage. "I watched you anchor. Your boat is so beautiful and elegant. Is it fast, as well?"

Charity looked at their yacht. "Not as fast as yours, but on a good day, I can sail over two hundred miles and not use a drop of fuel."

"Oh, that's not ours," Harper said. "Dad chartered it out of Cancun for a month for my graduation. We had five of my besties on board in Cancun for a week and now we're waiting for Dad to catch up. He's still back home in New Orleans." She paused and rolled her eyes. "Working."

"Well, we won't keep you," Suzette said. "Please give them our best when you see them. They left so abruptly after the shooting."

Charity turned to Karina. "Yes, I meant to ask about that. Harald said the trawler left to the north? I wonder why Savannah would go so soon after if it was thought to be dangerous?"

"Yes, it was," Karina replied. "It has been lurking around this area for some time and never answers hails from other boats. She probably figured it was best to leave and not expose her son to it."

That seems not only logical but prudent, Charity thought. The description of the trawler—rust stains and hanging tires—made Charity think it would be slower than Savannah's boat. Though *Sea Biscuit* wasn't fast by any means, her twin diesels were well-maintained and, at top speed, she felt sure Savannah could outrun the suspected cartel boat.

A single woman with a small boy would want to avoid conflict and anything that *invited* conflict. If the derelict-looking trawler actually *was* a cartel boat and it was hanging around in the area, leaving the same direction it went would be what Charity would have done.

They all said their goodbyes, then Charity climbed down and started her dinghy. After Harald untied the line and tossed it onto the deck, she pushed the little boat away from the junk and headed back to *Wind Dancer*.

Once aboard, she went below and prepared something she

could eat quickly before getting underway, then went forward, removed her clothes, and climbed into her bed.

Charity usually never had trouble falling asleep when she wanted to. Sailing meant following tides, weather, and current a lot more than the time of day.

She checked the forecast on her phone, and seeing nothing that would slow her, closed her eyes and was soon asleep.

Charity submerged in the shallow water as soon as she heard the siren and began to put her gear on. Jesse soon dropped below the surface beside her, putting on his second fin.

He looked at her and she nodded, then he struck out, swimming hard, as the bottom fell away below them.

No more than five minutes earlier, Charity had taken a man's life, as had Jesse. To compound that, they were illegally in a foreign country, having come ashore without clearing customs.

Charity moved along beside Jesse, staying back just enough to keep him in her field of vision and allowing him to see her peripherally with a slight turn of the head.

She checked her depth gauge—fifteen feet. Deep enough to avoid anything on the surface, but not so deep the ambient light from the moon and stars didn't reach.

The waitress had probably run inside and called the Royal Bahamas Police Force to report a shooting on the beach. They had a station just a short distance from the resort where she and Jesse had caught up to Paladin and killed him and his cohort.

She turned her head to watch Jesse swim. As big as he was, in the water, he moved fast when he wanted to. He kept his body streamlined, arms and gear tucked in. His powerful legs scissored the water, while the rest of his body stayed laser-straight, propelled headfirst into the darkness. His motions were almost machine-like in their precision.

"Do the masks work without the earwigs?" she asked.

"Yeah," Jesse replied. "But the range is even more limited. Stay close."

"Were you really going to bring them back?"

"No," he replied, then paused. "I just didn't want them to know what was going to happen."

She continued swimming in silence for a moment, then said, "Savannah didn't want you to do it."

"I was reluctant," he admitted. "I knew the man. *We* knew him. But after we heard his confession and promise to kill more, and Savannah agreeing he needed to be brought to justice, I knew it was the only way."

Charity didn't say anything for a moment. She saw Jesse turn his head to the left, then look back to his right, where she swam with her shoulder close to his hip.

"Jesse," Charity said softly. "Savannah wasn't on the comm when Chyrel picked up that phone call we heard."

They continued in silence for ten minutes, not slowing the pace in the slightest. Then Jesse stopped.

"Wait here," he said, then ascended to the surface.

With his head above water, he turned completely around before coming back down to Charity's depth.

"We passed the *Revenge*," he said, swimming slowly back the way they'd come. "This way."

Once they reached the boat, they quickly removed their gear in the water, slinging everything up onto the swim platform before climbing aboard. Then they picked everything up and stepped up through the transom door to the cockpit.

"You need to let the others know what happened," Charity said, her chest still heaving from the arduous swim. "They're probably worried."

Jesse's breathing was coming in rasps also, his wet shirt clinging to his body as his chest rose and fell. When he went to step past her, she put a hand against his chest.

They stood looking at one another for a long moment, then Charity made her decision. It was now or never.

Her hand went from his chest to the back of his neck as she pulled him into her embrace. They kissed passionately as she turned and stumbled onto the boat's fighting chair, where she sprawled backward, laughing, as Jesse pulled his shirt over his head, then fell on top of her.

Charity woke with a start, breathing heavily and drenched in sweat.

"Dammit!" she called out, slamming the heel of her fist into the mattress. "It didn't happen like that!"

She sat on the edge of her bunk, leaned forward and rubbed her face vigorously, as if she could scrub the thoughts from her mind.

Arching her spine, she pushed her hair back, tilted her face toward the moon shining through the open porthole and screamed, "We didn't do that!"

Why was she having these dreams? She'd almost rather have the nightmares. Why did she do what she did? Why did she have such feelings for this man? Jesse was a friend. A good friend. That was it.

And so was Savannah. These thoughts, these *transgressions*, they crossed a line she had vowed never to cross. Why was she plagued with these... feelings?

For years, Charity had been able to suppress her emotions and feelings, locking them up in an inactive part of her subconscious mind—the same place the demons dwelled.

Her sometimes-flirtatious attitude toward not only Jesse, but other men as well, was simply her way of behaving the way she thought a normal woman of her age and energy level should.

The trouble was, without emotion or feeling to direct her method of appearing normal—a facade created by the tactical part of her mind—her behavior might easily be misinterpreted.

She drew in a breath, held it, then slowly exhaled, trying to get a grip.

I can't help you if you're not honest with yourself first.

A voice from her past—a therapist she'd been ordered to see after Afghanistan. The first of many.

What was the honest truth? That she loved Jesse? She didn't think that emotion was available to her anymore. But even if she did, love and lust— well, those were different. Separate.

Sex was separate. Sex was what people did to feel good, to escape, to... get off.

Charity pushed those thoughts down and picked her watch up from the shelf. It was half past eleven and her alarm would be going off in thirty minutes.

She'd slept six hours and should have felt moderately refreshed. Seven hours was good for her, eight was perfect. But she'd often functioned for days on end with no more than power naps at the helm.

But she didn't feel refreshed at all. Charity knew that it was the emotional side that was stressed, and that her body had, in fact, rested sufficiently.

Her mind? Well, she could just turn that off during the trip up the coast.

She dressed quickly, then went through the same routine she normally did first thing in the morning.

Six minutes of preparation and cooking, then four minutes eating the omelet and drinking a bottle of water, and two minutes cleaning the dishes.

With nothing left to do, she sat down at the navigation desk and pulled up the chart plotter on her laptop to begin plotting her course to Progreso, and to look more closely at the coastline for possible spots Savannah might have stopped. There were a few locations that looked good, the nearest just fifty-five nautical miles away.

If she weren't in a hurry, ten hours at six knots would be a casual day cruise for *Sea Biscuit*. So, if she stopped there and didn't leave until sunrise, Charity could be within ten or twelve miles when Savannah got underway.

And if they maintained the two-knot closure speed Charity estimated, she might possibly overtake *Sea Biscuit* by noon.

Tomorrow, she resolved. *I'll finally talk to Savannah tomorrow.*

# CHAPTER SEVEN

Seated at a small outdoor table in the shade, a Hispanic man looked out over the tranquil turquoise waters of the Bay of Campeche. On the table was a half-empty can of Coke, an ashtray, a pack of American cigarettes, a small notepad and pen, and a pair of binoculars.

The man didn't appear out of place, and there really weren't many people around who would see him, anyway. He was slightly built but tall, with more European features than the mostly indigenous population in the area. He had tattoos on his neck, depicting a giant snake and a crocodile facing one another with vicious intent.

He picked up the binoculars and trained them on a large yacht anchored no more than half a mile from shore. Then he put them down and made a note on his pad.

The target was a twenty-two-year-old college student, vacationing with her mother. Luis looked down at his phone again. The photo of the woman displayed on it was quite beautiful with long dark hair and dark eyes– *mamacíta!*

The mother and daughter were aboard an eighty-foot Azimut yacht called *MollySue*, and, according to Luis's sources, they'd arrived a week earlier.

When the yacht had arrived, it had meant nothing to Luis—just another bunch of *turistas*. But Luis was informed of the arrival of any boat, no matter how large or how small. The same went for new people arriving by car. Vacationers on airplanes and cruise ships were of no interest, but people traveling alone might mean rivals trying to move into his area.

Like the *barco decrépito* that had fired on him and his men as they went to investigate what they were doing.

But then Luis had received orders from *El Jefe*, who was in his mountain stronghold in Morelos, not far from Mexico City. He'd sent the picture, the woman's name, and orders to kidnap her within four days.

Since receiving the direct call from the cartel boss, Luis had had men watching the yacht, and he, himself, had been keeping an eye on it all morning.

As far as they could tell, the target liked to stay up late, lounging on the aft deck, and listening to music on her phone until long after the *puta madre* and crew had gone to bed.

He hoped tonight she would do the same. It would make for easier retrieval.

When he'd first set eyes on the yacht, he'd grumbled to his *teniente;* neither man liked boats.

Luis hated the water, always had. A nice hotel, a grab at the plaza, or even from one of those short-term rentals that were so popular with tourists. Anywhere would be better than abducting the woman from a boat.

Not to mention the risk involved.

No, grabbing her from the yacht was going to be a real pain in the ass. He shook his head. *Malditos Americanos ricos.*

Luis had only been sent to Campeche two months earlier, to

organize local gangs and spread the control of *Cártel del Pacífico Sur* from the west coast to the east. Mateo had arrived shortly after, coming down from the central part of Sinaloa.

They'd needed to recruit some help for this job and had to barter for the use of a quiet fishing boat. Then he and Mateo had to come up with a plan for not just the grab, but for where they'd come ashore, and where they'd stash the van. It was riskier than the usual retrieval. But this one would have big rewards. At least *El Jefe* said it would.

The boss had called Luis directly, which rarely happened. This was a high- value target, to be taken *alive*—no fuck-ups. One mistake and his head would be on the chopping block.

It went without saying. You couldn't say no to the boss. Whatever he demanded, you did. Didn't matter if you'd never set foot on a boat before, or if it was your cousin's wedding, or your daughter's *quinceañera*. If *El Jefe* called, you answered.

At least the weather would be good. That was the first thing he checked. The moon would be nearly full and high overhead at midnight, but a layer of high, dense clouds was supposed to move in after sunset and would all but block the moon out. He'd have preferred the total darkness of a new moon—you always went under cover of darkness if you could—but there was no leeway in the timing. If the clouds didn't come, they'd move ahead anyway. It had to be tonight. With that rig, they could pull anchor any time and be miles down the coast, hours away, making an already difficult job a logistical nightmare.

A new boat had appeared on the horizon and was now entering the anchorage. He raised the binoculars he'd bought earlier that day at a tourist shop to assess the situation. It was an old sailboat with what appeared to be a woman at the helm. As the boat got closer,

Luis saw that it was definitely a woman. She was wearing a bikini top and tan shorts.

She looked like the typical American blonde, all the money to travel to Mexico but too stupid or too arrogant to even learn how to say thank you in Spanish.

But as he watched, his assessment changed. She handled her boat like a professional. Very quickly, she had the anchor set and the sails down. And all by herself, too. Once she'd disappeared below deck, he shifted his attention back to the big motor yacht.

Just a few minutes later, he heard an outboard and moved the binoculars toward the source of the sound.

The blonde from the sailboat was in her dinghy and motoring over to the next boat.

Another boating *turista*.

He set the binoculars down and took a sip of his Coke. Sometimes these jobs were so boring. It was all the waiting. The only thing more boring than some of the people's lives he'd surveilled over the years was watching those people live those boring lives, minute by minute—now she was making a sandwich, now she was going to the bathroom, now she was flipping through a magazine... All the while the boring target had no idea what was to come.

It gave Luis satisfaction, knowing he held someone's future in his hands, knowing their fate, controlling the unwitting like a *marioneta*.

Who else could say that?

No el padre en la misión, he thought. The man couldn't even keep his congregation from straying.

Soon, the sun would go down, the wheels would be set in motion, and there would be no turning back.

The rich American college girl's fate would be sealed.

Everything would have to go as he'd planned. Luis liked his jobs neat and clean—no additional casualties and no complications. He ran a tight crew.

But that was on his usual jobs—this one was more complicated. He worried he hadn't thought of all the possible scenarios. He'd have to trust his men to do what they'd been told, something he didn't find easy.

The high-pitched whir of an outboard motor caught his attention. A small fishing boat, he thought someone had called it a Whaler, zipped along the shore from the south. Mateo was at the helm.

Luis rose from his chair as his *teniente* ran the bow of the boat right up on shore, killing the engine mere feet from where Luis stood,

Luis staggered backward, yelling in Spanish, "What the hell, man?"

Mateo shrugged.

Luis scowled. "I don't need you drawing attention."

"Are you kidding?" Mateo grinned. "This is how everyone drives around here. If I didn't, *that* would draw attention." He slapped Luis on the arm with the back of his hand. "You worry too much, *amigo.*"

And my second-in-command is becoming too familiar, Luis thought. "Perhaps," he said, fixing Mateo with a cold stare. "But I always succeed."

Mateo nodded. He couldn't argue that.

"Are the others on their way? The van in place?"

"Just as you ordered, *jefe.*"

"Good." Luis calmed. He was a little jumpy, still on edge from his conversation with *El Jefe.* "You remember your part?"

"*Si.*"

"Let me hear it."

"Again?"

"Again."

Mateo let loose a huff before beginning. "When you give the word, I drive at idle speed toward the big *yate*. Once we are close, I flicker the running lights, then turn them off, so if anyone is watching, it looks like they've gone out due to an electrical malfunction. Once we reach the back of the boat, I do not tie a line. I keep the engine running and hold on to a cleat or something while the others board and then return. Then we haul ass, *muy rápido*, to the van, leaving this boat on shore. It will be reported stolen tomorrow morning."

Luis nodded. The man made it sound simple. Hopefully, it would be. But Luis had been around long enough to know that as soon as you let your guard down, you'd get a bite right in the ass.

"And the safe houses?" Luis asked.

"Three of them now," Mateo replied. "We found another great place just today, abandoned for years."

"We'll take the target to the one near the park first," Luis said, then drained the last of the Coke and tossed the empty bottle in a trash can. "In the morning, we will move her to the second one and you and I will go investigate this third one."

"Hey, I'm a professional," Mateo said. "I may look like a beach bum, but that's the point, no?"

The rest of the crew, Juan and David, sauntered toward them in swimming trunks. Juan carried a volleyball and David had a six-pack cooler.

"See what I mean?" Mateo said.

They looked like they didn't have a care in the world.

Bueno.

The sun was already bathing the palm trees in orange and gold. Soon it would be dark. And they would wait.

Two hours later, after watching the target and her mother leave the big yacht, then return an hour later, Luis relaxed a little. They'd gone over to the large sailboat at the other end of the anchorage to visit the Dutch couple.

The odd-looking sailboat had been hanging around for a long time. Luis was aware of everything about the Dutch couple and knew they were harmless, but it had troubled him that the target had left the yacht and he was uneasy until she'd returned. He knew what they'd be up against on the yacht—an older, fat captain, two crewmen, and a cook—nothing his men couldn't handle if they had to. The plan was not to have to. Grab the girl off the back of the boat and be gone before anyone even got out of bed. With luck, they wouldn't even know until morning.

Luis watched through the binoculars as one, then another light was turned off in the cabins aboard the *MollySue.*

He waited another hour and a half. The target had been going to bed after midnight for the last several nights. It was eleven-thirty. This was it.

He told his men to push the Whaler back from shore; they all climbed aboard, and Mateo started the outboard, which, at idle, was very quiet.

To Luis, it seemed the yacht was a great distance from shore, and he started to think they should have left earlier. But before his worry turned to panic, Mateo was flipping the nav light switch on and off, and then he killed the lights. David laughed softly, looking toward the yacht with an expression of glee.

Moments later, they eased up to the stern of the big yacht. The girl was looking the other way, headphones connected to her cell phone.

Luis grinned, but there was no mirth in his expression.

Suddenly, there was a noise from above, and Luis was instantly bathed in a bright light.

CHAPTER EIGHT

Charity closed the navigation computer and tented her fingers under her chin. She was feeling more apprehensive than ever, knowing that sometime tomorrow, she would probably sight *Sea Biscuit.*

Suddenly, a gunshot rang out, the sound reverberating across the water.

Charity instinctively dropped to the deck beside the nav desk. Reaching up under the lid of the desk, she found the catch and opened the hiding spot by feel.

The Diamondback DB9 semi-automatic that was stashed there dropped into her palm. It had a very reassuring feel.

The shot had come from her boat's port side, to the north. She estimated it was two hundred yards away, but sound waves traveling over the surface of water could make noises seem as if they were much closer than they were. It was definitely a large caliber rifle.

People started shouting, but she couldn't make out what anyone was saying.

The commotion seemed to be coming from another vessel in the anchorage, but she wasn't sure which one, only that there were several angry voices and at least one frightened female voice, both abruptly punctuated by a loud scream.

Whatever was going on, it was too far away to be an immediate threat to her, so she rose and slid back into the seat. Too far to be an immediate threat also meant too far for any quick action on her part.

She moved the navigation computer aside and lifted the desk's lid. The flat screen monitor on the underside flickered to life, showing night-optic camera views of several parts of her boat.

There was nobody on *Wind Dancer's* decks or nearby. She clenched her teeth, frustrated.

Just what I need, she thought. She had one mission—to find Savannah. And now this. Whatever it was, if she pulled anchor and set sail now, she'd have the local LEOs chasing her down, asking questions.

Though she was closer than she'd ever been, there was no leaving now. She would be delayed.

She toggled the mast cam, raising the angle and turning it toward where she thought the sound of the commotion was coming from.

Barely visible red lights showed from the windows of the forward house on the junk. Beyond it, the power cat was fully illuminated, but she saw no movement on deck or anywhere around it. The small sloop was dark. Beyond that, lights were coming on aboard *MollySue* and the flybridge spotlight was pointing almost straight up in the air.

"What the hell's going on?" Charity asked aloud, then reached over and turned on the VHF.

She could see activity at the stern and zoomed the camera in. Two men were dragging the young woman she'd met earlier down the yacht's steps and onto the swim platform.

Dammit.

Charity knew what that meant. A small boat was waiting, and two more men quickly wrestled Harper aboard.

A kidnapping.

Then the others jumped in, and the small boat sped away into the darkness with no lights on.

The men were in an eighteen- to twenty-foot Whaler with what looked like about a two-hundred-horse outboard engine. There was no way she could chase it in her dinghy. Especially not with a half-a-mile head start and them angling away from her.

She tracked the boat until it disappeared near shore, made note of the exact location, then moved the camera back to *MollySue*.

"What is happening?" a woman's voice came over the VHF. "Does anybody know?"

It was Karina on *Lange Reis*, the junk next to her. Charity looked through *Dancer's* small windows and could see a single light shining through one of the junk's round, forward portholes. A shadow passed in front of it.

Charity keyed the microphone. "I think it came from the other end of the anchorage."

"I heard it too," a man said. "I think she's right. The sound came from down near *MollySue*. But it's so dark I can't see anything."

Charity assumed the man speaking was aboard either the Powercat or the small, dark sloop anchored beyond *Lange Reis*.

"*MollySue*, *MollySue*, this is *Lange Reis*." Karina hailed on the radio. "Are you all right?"

There was no reply for a moment, then an excited male voice came over the radio speaker. "We have been attacked! Mayday! Mayday! Mayday! This is the motor vessel *MollySue*, anchored one kilometer off Campeche dock. We have been attacked and boarded. One crewman is seriously injured and one passenger has been abducted— Harper Landry!"

There were two types of emergency calls at sea. Both were to be taken seriously by any mariners in the immediate area. A Pan-Pan was issued when a vessel needed assistance, but it wasn't life threatening. But when a Mayday went out, that meant there was imminent danger of loss of life and any and all mariners in the area were to render assistance if at all possible without compounding the situation.

But this was different. It wasn't a vessel taking on water with inadequate life jackets aboard. This involved gunfire.

Charity opened the gun's hiding spot again and withdrew her holster, inserted the DB9 in it, and clipped it on the inside of her pants on her right hip. She pulled her shirt over it, but the bulge left no doubt what was under her shirt.

Then she retrieved a stack of four small, leather-bound cases, opening the top one—a passport issued to Gabriela Ortiz-Fleming, which she used when posing as an editor for Tropical Luxury Magazine. She thrust it into her pocket and started to put the others back, then thought better of it and opened the second one—her badge and Homeland Security ID. The third one was a passport, also in her own name. She dropped those in the opposite pocket and then put the last booklet back and closed the compartment.

She grabbed her handheld VHF and started up the ladder. "I am coming to assist," she announced, her voice commanding. "Everyone else, stay put. *MollySue*, have all the pirates left?"

"Yes," the man replied. "Who are you and how can you help?"

Charity quickly punched the numbers into the keypad to disarm and unlock the overhead hatch, then she shoved it back and scrambled up to the deck.

She keyed the mic again. "I can keep them from coming back," she said, pulling her dinghy alongside and dropping into it.

The engine caught on the first pull, and she yanked the bitter end of the painter, loosening the knot, then twisted the throttle.

The little rigid-hulled inflatable accelerated quickly. Charity steered around the stern of *Lange Reis*, then rocketed across the calm water toward the large motor yacht, keeping an eye out in the direction the kidnappers had disappeared.

She reached the stern quickly and saw a man in uniform up in the covered aft cockpit with Suzette. "Suzette," she called out to her, "is everyone okay?"

The woman looked down, then moved over to the rail. "They took Harper!"

Charity quickly tied off and jumped over to the yacht, not bothering to ask permission. She charged up the steps and saw the girl's mother, now sitting in a deck chair, sobbing.

Charity looked over at the captain and approached him. "I heard a gunshot. Was anyone hurt?"

"The night watch," he replied, pointing toward the flybridge ladder. "He's been shot."

Not wanting to involve herself with a hysterical mother just yet, Charity turned and headed over to the ladder.

"How can *you* stop them?" Suzette asked.

Charity paused, one foot on the ladder. "I'm an armed woman with an attitude, and I was once in Harper's situation."

She went straight up the steps to the flybridge, where she found a young man lying on the deck next to the spotlight.

She checked his neck for a pulse, though his vacant eyes told her there'd be none.

What a shame, she thought, closing his eyes. *So young.*

Then she rose, switched off the spotlight, and went back down to the cockpit as two other dinghies approached.

Suzette continued to sob into her hands.

Charity turned toward the captain. "Did you reach S.A.R. or the police?"

"Nothing from Search and Rescue," he replied. "The Campeche police are sending a boat. Who are you? And why are you armed?"

He sounded American, but didn't have any discernable accent. Charity studied the man's face for a moment. "My name isn't important, but you can call me Gabby. I am a former police officer in Miami."

"I see," he said. "And that gives you the right to board my vessel with a gun in Mexico?"

She fixed the man with a cold glare. "I imagine your dead crewman up there was about to ask those pirates the same question when they shot him. Look at the trouble it got him."

The color drained from the captain's face. "He's... dead?"

"Yes," Charity replied, still staring at him with eyes of ice. "Bullet to the chest—7.62, if I had to guess. It sounded like an AK."

"He... said he was okay," the captain croaked, his eyes becoming somewhat vacant. "Said to take care of the passengers."

"Who else is aboard?"

"Huh?"

She took the captain's arm and turned him away from Suzette, tightly squeezing the tendon connecting the triceps to the elbow. That got his attention.

"I need you to step up, Captain," she hissed quietly. "You have a man down and a young woman missing, and her hysterical mother to deal with. Nothing can be done for him. Now, who else is aboard?"

"Another crewman," he replied. "And my wife, who is the chef."

"Where are they now?"

He glanced toward the massive wall of glass separating the cockpit from the interior. "I told them to stay in their cabins. The crewman... is also young."

"Smart thinking," Charity said, as the first dinghy reached *MollySue's* stern. Karina was kneeling in the front with the line in her hand.

"Is it safe to come aboard?" she called up.

"Yes," Charity replied, then turned back to the captain. "Why don't you go and tell them it's safe to come out now. Karina and I will stay with Suzette."

He disappeared into the cabin as Karina and Harald came quickly up the steps.

"What happened?" Karina asked, looking at Suzette with fear in her eyes. "Was it Harper?"

"Yes," Charity replied. "Go to her. She needs you."

Then she turned to Harald. "There is a dead man up on the flybridge. Can you find a blanket or something to cover the body?"

"I have an... emergency blanket, in the... er..."

"*Bijboot?*" Charity asked with a wink.

He grinned. "*Ja!* I will take care of it."

He disappeared down the steps, passing a young couple from yet another dinghy as they were coming up. The woman went past Charity without a word, knowing only that her friend needed help.

"My name's Trevor," the man said. "What happened?"

"You're on the Leopard?" she asked, referring to the power catamaran.

He nodded.

"Suzette's daughter, Harper, has been kidnapped," Charity explained. "One of the crew was killed."

"Killed? What's going on?"

Harald came back up carrying a folded silver blanket.

"Just cover the body," Charity told him. "Don't move or touch anything."

He nodded and went up the steps.

"You seem as if you're no stranger to this kind of thing," Trevor said, looking over at his wife and Karina huddled around Suzette.

His accent, though he managed to conceal most of it, made him an obvious New Englander.

"Unfortunately," she said with a heavy sigh.

He looked at Charity for a long moment before asking, "Former military?"

She nodded. "And law enforcement."

"Are Mexican authorities coming?"

"The captain said they were," Charity replied. "I don't know if you know much about how things work south of the border, but I'm not expecting them to be of much help."

He nodded somberly. "I'm afraid you're right."

There was a pinging sound, like her cell phone, but it was coming from where the three women were sitting. Suzette picked up her phone and looked at it. Then, for a brief moment, the smallest of smiles crossed her face.

CHAPTER NINE

Savannah lay awake in her bed, staring up at the ceiling in the darkness. She couldn't see the details but knew where everything was located. Just above her left shoulder was a place in the underside of the gelcoat where the weave of the fiberglass was barely visible.

She'd told herself for years that she was going to correct the flaw—it was cosmetic and had nothing to do with structural integrity—but had just never gotten around to doing it.

Above her knees, Savannah could barely make out the center beam that Jesse had always hit his head on.

The desire to go back to him was strong, but she hadn't yet worked things out in her mind. She had her own way of doing things and did them in her own time. She always had and probably always would.

The fact that she was now married, and had been for several years, didn't alter the fact.

Living aboard *Sea Biscuit* all those years, just she and Flo, she'd steered a wide course around trouble, and when danger presented itself, she ran if she could.

Her tanks never got below half-full the whole time Flo was going from toddler to teenager, and the engines, generator, water maker, and other systems were serviced regularly.

Sea Biscuit wasn't the fastest boat on the water, but with the recent engine changes Jesse had completed, she could travel two hundred miles in just ten hours before needing fuel, or six times that distance while at a comfortable trawler speed of six knots, slipping slowly from cove to cove for weeks at a time in the Bahamas.

With her long range, low profile, and shallow draft, *Sea Biscuit* was the queen of hide-and-seek, and Savannah had relied on her boat's speed and range to get her out of many bad situations before it became too late.

It had reached a point where she'd seen a bit too much of the ugly side of Jesse's life and she didn't like it. He'd always come out on top so far, but one day he wouldn't. Was she selfish to think she and Alberto might become collateral damage when that happened?

He'd killed a man in cold blood.

He'd set out to find and kill him and that's exactly what he'd done.

So, Savannah had run. It had been her fallback tactic for so long, she was ten miles out to sea before even thinking of the repercussions. That was when she'd first called Flo. Her daughter had understood her need to run and hadn't asked questions. Savannah had simply told her that something had gone wrong on one of Jesse's ops, but he was fine, and she just needed some sea time.

That had been their code phrase for alone time since Flo was a little girl. Either of them could announce at any time that they needed some sea time, and they'd get underway. Then, whoever needed to be alone—usually Savannah—would pilot *Sea Biscuit* from the flybridge until she worked out in her mind what was bothering her.

LIABLE CHARITY

Savannah had been working it out for almost four months and still hadn't come to any conclusion other than that she missed Jesse.

She'd left the anchorage in Campeche when the Dutch woman started asking questions she didn't want to explain or lie about. She and her husband were nice enough, but a little too prying.

The New Orleans woman and her daughter had been better company. Southerners tended not to pry nearly as much, and the daughter was great company for Alberto. He was at that in-between age, when girls didn't seem so yucky, but he was still nervous and awkward talking to them. She was twice his age, a grown woman, but was able to relate to him and, she truly seemed to enjoy his company.

The girl had just graduated with a teaching degree and her mother was so proud that Harper had landed a job at the same public elementary school she'd attended as a child.

Suzette's husband was a judge and was supposed to join them the day after Savannah left. From her conversations with both Suzette and Harper, it seemed they lived far below their means and did a lot of charitable work. Savannah had liked them.

Progreso was still two days away, but if she didn't get some sleep, it could be three or four. But they were in no hurry. Her friend from back home wouldn't be arriving there until Friday afternoon, nearly a week away.

Nikki was almost a year older than her, but they'd graduated high school together and, though they were of different races, they were the best of friends. Their fathers had worked together when they were younger and when Savannah's dad bought his second boat, Nikki's father became the captain.

A month ago, while Savannah had been thinking about her days back in Beaufort, she'd decided to look Nikki up. She had been surprisingly easy to locate—she lived in her parents' old house on nearby St. Helena Island and, more than three decades later, even had the same phone number.

Nikki had been thrilled to hear from her and even more thrilled to learn she was in the Yucatan. She and her husband had been planning a two-week summer vacation in Progreso for the kids' summer break.

For Savannah, it would be a comforting trip to her past. She glanced at her watch and saw that it was almost midnight. The watch would be alerting her to make a check up on deck in just a few minutes anyway, so she rose from the bed and quietly opened the aft hatch to the cockpit.

When she reached the small flybridge, she sat down at the helm and, out of habit, switched on the VHF to catch the midnight weather update.

Looking around, she saw nothing but water and the beach half a mile away, but even that was only barely visible. A quick glance at the sky told her why.

The forecasted cloudiness had arrived. There was no chance of rain or wind associated with it, just a high dense cover of cirrus clouds that would hide the sun, moon, and stars for the next couple of days.

The radio crackled and she heard a garbled urgent broadcast filled with static. "We have been *shhhh! Shhhh*-day! Mayday! *Shhhhhh!* This is the *shhhhhhhhhh MollySue*, anchored *shhhhhhhhhhhh* off Campeche dock. We *shhhhhhhh* attacked and boarded. One crewman is *shhhhhhh* injured and one passenger has been abducted, Harper *shhhhh!*"

Harper Landry? Abducted? Oh my God!

She'd just hugged the young woman goodbye less than a day ago.

Poor Suzette!

Hundreds of miles from home and her husband stuck working in New Orleans. She must be terrified.

Savannah knew all too well what it felt like to have her daughter snatched from thin air and carried off by God-knew-who. The familiar panic rushed through her veins at the thought.

Savannah made up her mind instantly and hurried back down to the salon.

"Alberto, wake up!" she called down to the forward cabin. "We have to go."

"Huh?" a sleepy voice came from the open door.

"I need your help, sweetie," Savannah said, then turned the key and pressed both starter buttons.

As Alberto came out of the forward cabin, trudging up the steps in his pajamas, the twin diesel engines rumbled to life.

"What's going on?" he asked, alert now that the engines were running.

"We have to go back to Campeche," Savannah said. "And I'm going to need your help. Go get dressed. Quick like a bunny, now."

He hurried down the steps and Savannah removed her phone from the charger. She and Suzette had exchanged numbers. She wrote a quick text to her new friend.

Heard the Mayday. Heading back. Be there asap.

She hit the *Send* button, then began checking the engine instruments.

"Why do we have to go back?" Alberto asked, returning to the lower helm fully dressed. "What's wrong?"

Savannah looked over at her adopted son. For several years, she and Jesse had tried to shield him from the ugliness in the world. She, more than him. At times, it seemed as if the ugliness in the world

81

sought Jesse out—targeting him for some reason.

Alberto had lost both his parents to violence and drugs when he was eight. It had never escaped Savannah's attention that Jesse too, had lost his parents at that age. But unlike him, Alberto hadn't had caring grandparents to raise him.

In the end, there just wasn't any way to shield him from all of it, as that was the line of work Jesse was engaged in.

And that was the reason she'd left. To remove violence from Alberto's life. Or so she'd thought. Nothing else had mattered, except that he be allowed to grow up knowing only love. Jesse's own actions, covert as they may have been, were robbing the boy of the one constant Jesse himself had experienced growing up—innocence.

"There's a problem back there," Savannah said, plotting a course but having trouble getting the chart plotter to cooperate.

"Let me," Alberto said, then stepped in front of the plotter.

Though he'd only turned eleven a few weeks earlier, Alberto had spent the bulk of the last three years at sea with her and Jesse. He was more than capable of spelling her if she needed a short nap on the long, comfortable couch right behind the lower helm.

Besides, all he'd have to do was keep his eyes open and the autopilot would do the rest.

A few seconds later, he looked up and grinned. "Course laid in, Captain."

She smiled at him. "Good job, Navigator."

She paused and looked into his dark eyes, wondering how to tell him.

Alberto stepped back from the chart plotter and crossed his arms like Jesse did when he wanted answers. "What happened, Mom?"

"Harper Landry has been kidnapped and we're going back to help."

"Kidnapped? You mean taken away? But why? By who?"

"I don't know, sweetie. But we're going to go back and help in any capacity we can."

He nodded his head resolutely. "But why would someone take Harper?"

"I don't know."

The despair in his eyes tore at her heart. He knew what being kidnapped meant. As his face started to scrunch up and his eyes welled with tears, she pulled him to her chest.

"I know you want to cry," she whispered. "It's okay. I do, too. But right now, we are going to get this boat in gear, and go help. Right?"

He nodded, wiping his eyes. "Right."

Out of habit, Savannah switched on the primary VHF. Its antenna was mounted at the top of the radar mast, ten feet higher than the less powerful radio on the flybridge.

Alberto brought up the radar overlay on the chart plotter. "I don't see anything for at least eight miles," he said, looking up at her. "And the course is deep all the way there."

"Just like coming up here this morning," she agreed. "We can hot bunk on the couch. If I get too tired, can you can give me a break for a short nap?"

"What will I have to do?"

"With luck, nothing at all," she replied. "You've sat a watch with me or Dad or one of *Ambrosia's* crew before. Just sit here and watch out for whales or floating logs. If you see anything, just wake me."

"I can do that," he said. "Want me to go get the bridle off?"

"Be careful," Savannah replied. "It's dark and the deck might—"

"Be slippery. I know."

He went through the hatch and up to the foredeck, where he quickly hauled in the starboard bridle and unhooked the chain anchor rode, which splashed into the water. Then, he removed the bridle from the two forward cleats and put it away before pulling the water hose out of the chain locker.

"All set," he called back to her, turning the water on for a second to make sure it worked.

Savannah bumped the starboard engine into forward for a moment, then toggled the anchor windlass. The rode began to clank across the rollers as Alberto directed the spray onto the links, rinsing the saltwater and any sand from the chain.

Once the anchor came up and was seated, he attached the safety chain, then sprayed the anchor down, as Savannah put both transmissions in forward and turned the boat south.

When he finished, Alberto put the hose away and came back to the helm. Savannah hopped up onto the helm seat so he could get past her.

"What's going to happen to Harper?" he asked, the worry evident in his words.

The radio crackled for a second, then Savannah heard a familiar voice. "I am coming to assist. Everyone else stay put. *MollySue*, have all the pirates left?"

Alberto looked up at her, surprise evident in his eyes. "That was Aunt Charity!"

A million things ran through Savannah's mind, not the least of which was the idea that Jesse had sent Charity to find her.

She'd told him explicitly in her letter that he was neither to come looking for her nor send anyone.

The thought made her angry.

She just needed time. Safe time. She rubbed her left shoulder where she'd been shot helping Jesse with an investigation in Key West.

Safe time away from her husband, who was a magnet for violence, and for some inexplicable reason, never stepped out of its path. It was as though he thrived on it.

But the one thing that stood out in Savannah's mind the most, as soon as she'd heard Charity's take-charge, no-nonsense voice, was that she was the best person to be there and deal with the immediate fallout of what had apparently happened—the kidnapping of an American judge's daughter for ransom.

But would Charity alone be able to handle it?

Savannah had heard of kidnappings in other parts of Mexico and knew the police weren't of much help.

She reached for her phone again and pulled up the number of someone she was sure could help, and who Charity would know.

"Livingston," Deuce replied after the first ring,

She paused for a second, unsure just what to say to him.

"Hello?"

"Deuce, it's Savannah. Please don't tell Jesse we talked. But I need your help."

His reply was immediate. "Name it."

"There's a situation in Mexico. An American girl—a friend's daughter—has been kidnapped."

Finding out Charity's reason for being there would have to wait.

# CHAPTER TEN

When the police boat from Campeche arrived, Charity knew there was little chance of anything of consequence being done to help find the girl. Neither of the two responding police officers wore any kind of rank insignia—basic patrolmen answering a disturbance call.

Kidnappings for ransom happened all the time and the fastest resolution was to pay the ransom. Shootings were becoming all too common, as well. In this case, both had occurred, and yet the only response from the police was to send a couple of lowly officers.

Thanks for your assistance. The coroner will be out in the morning to collect the body. If you remember anything, give us a call.

The procedure was basically the same as in Miami, but nothing moved fast in Mexico.

They did at least go through the motions and asked all the right questions of everyone on board.

The young crewman who'd been hiding below deck had said he'd looked out a window and saw one of the men on the boat clearly when the spotlight went on.

"He had... tattoos on both sides of his neck—*un cocodrilo y una serpiente.*"

When the younger cop turned to his partner, Charity saw him

make the cross on his chest and noticed the clear anxiety in his eyes.

Crocodile and snake tattoos? Those were some easily identifiable marks.

Something told Charity this guy wasn't trying to hide very hard, and that was troublesome.

Another tick in the "Not Good" column.

Exposing herself as a federal agent or even trying to use Armstrong Research's influence with local law enforcement probably wouldn't go over real well with these guys.

When the senior cop turned and asked for her ID, Charity handed him the phony passport. She'd moved the slim DB9 and holster to the small of her back before they'd boarded. It was completely inconspicuous there.

"*Mi nombre es* Gabriela Ortiz-Fleming," she said in fluent Spanish. "*Soy la editora de* Tropical Luxury Magazine."

"What did you see?" he asked in heavily accented English.

"Nothing," she lied, keeping the Whaler's location—her ace in the hole—close to her chest. "I heard a gunshot and came in reply to the Mayday."

He studied her passport for a moment, checked the entry stamp from three months ago, then handed it back. "You are friends with Señora Landry?"

Charity nodded, putting her passport back in her pocket. "Yes, I am."

"You must stay until we are finished," he said, then went over to the other cop and said something in a low voice to him, both staring at her.

She smiled. Maybe it would rattle their superiors' chains, maybe it wouldn't. Kidnappings were bad press in tourist destinations, and they had a travel magazine editor as an eyewitness to a kidnapping.

Or at least an earwitness.

"I don't think they're taking this very seriously," Trevor said, standing close to her but looking away.

"No, they're not." She looked over and appraised him more closely. He was tall and obviously fit, as was his wife. "You former military, too?"

He shook his head. "Hardly," he replied with a snicker. "We do a cruising vlog."

"Cruising vlog?"

"On YouTube," he replied. "Heather does most of the video stuff. We document our travels and post them for people to watch."

"A lot of people watch stuff like that?"

He grinned. "It's paid our way for a couple of years now, including the purchase of the Leopard. We have almost half a million subscribers. Did I hear you say you're with a magazine?"

"I *own* a magazine," she replied, watching the cops continue their talk with Suzette. "A travel magazine."

Trevor also turned and looked at them. "I think your occupation had a bigger impact than ours."

"Let's hope both do," Charity replied. "We need any help we can get."

One of the policemen handed Suzette a card and Charity knew what that meant. She'd done it herself a thousand times as a Miami cop—*call me if you remember anything.* They rarely did.

"I think they're leaving," Trevor said.

And just like that, the two cops went down the steps and got into their boat.

Charity went over to sit beside Suzette. "What did they say?"

The woman looked up at her with red, bloodshot eyes. "They said to let them know when the kidnappers make a ransom demand," she replied, seeming to be in shock. "They said it is always better to cooperate with the kidnappers."

"Unfortunately, that's usually the case," Charity said, feeling herself getting pulled more deeply into the situation. "A lot of Mexican police are in the cartels' pockets."

"You mean they might be in on this?"

"Not directly," Charity replied. "The cartels control the people and the police through violence and bribes. They'll look the other way if the cartel does anything illegal in the open. So will the people."

"But why Harper?" Suzette pleaded. "We're not wealthy by any means. What will happen if they ask for more than we have?"

"Let's hope it doesn't come to that," Charity replied, knowing full well that she had a king's ransom stashed on board her boat. "Right now, all we can do is wait."

"She used to be a cop," Trevor said, kneeling in front of Suzette.

Charity resolved to postpone finding Savannah, at least for tonight, and reached over to take the woman's hand. "I will help you through this."

Savannah would have to wait. But at least now Charity knew where she was going, and she could always start the search again from there if she didn't find her.

Right now, she had to do what she could to help this woman get her daughter back alive. Maybe with Trevor and Harald's help, she could go ashore in the morning and poke around a little. Both seemed like competent men. But how much danger could she put them in?

She left Suzette and took Karina and the captain aside. "All we can do is wait for a ransom call," she told them.

"They said the local coroner would be coming in the morning,"

90

the captain said, glancing toward the flybridge. "I don't know how I'm going to tell his family."

"Has Suzette called her husband?" Charity asked.

Karina nodded. "He's sending someone but can't come himself. He's hearing a very important case."

More important than his daughter's safety? Charity thought. *Hmm, another tick in the Not Good column.*

Charity nodded toward Suzette. "She needs sleep; she's emotionally exhausted. The rest of us can take turns keeping watch and listening by her phone in case the kidnappers call. Would you please make sure it's plugged in and fully charged?"

"We will both help," Karina said, nodding firmly.

Heather, who'd been standing nearby, turned and stepped up beside Karina. "Trevor and I will do all we can, too. That girl has such a bright future. But what can we do?"

During her travels, Charity had met people like these many times over—young cruisers who stuck together and helped one another.

She pulled the second small booklet out and opened it. "My name isn't Gabby Fleming. I'm Charity Styles, and I work for the Homeland Security Department of the United States."

"But what is an American federal agent doing here in Mexico?" Trevor asked, joining them.

Suzette rose, and having overheard the exchange, came and stood beside the captain, appearing more lucid. "Homeland Security? Did you know this might happen? Were you already watching these men?"

"No. I'm just a cruiser like you," she replied. "One who happens to work remotely for the government. But for this situation, I don't think that will help matters. Which is why I didn't identify myself to

91

the police."

"I don't understand," the captain said. "You suspect the police are involved? I'm not sure that warrants investigation by a foreign government."

"You're right, Captain," Charity agreed. "Have you ever heard of Armstrong Research?"

His eyes practically clicked as they locked onto hers. "You know people at Armstrong?"

It often amazed Charity how well-known the organization was in certain circles, and how it could still fly under the radar.

She smiled. "I answer only to the company's head of security, who answers only to Jack Armstrong."

"But what about your friend, Savannah?" Karina asked. "You said you were trying to find her."

"I am," Charity replied. "She's the closest friend I have, but, right now, this is more important. Every minute counts, so please excuse me."

She took her secure satellite phone from her pocket and stepped over to the starboard side for an unobstructed view to the southeast, where she hoped the Armstrong communications satellite was still locked in geosynchronous orbit.

Charity debated who to call. She could trust Chyrel, up until it involved relocation of assets, which she couldn't do without authorization.

Jesse was out.

Finally, she clicked on the entry for "An Old Fart" and waited.

She'd thought it funny when she'd edited the entry the phone had come with so that every time he'd call, the display would announce, "An Old Fart is Calling."

"You'd better have a damned good reason for calling me at zero-dark-thirty, Captain," retired Colonel Travis Stockwell growled.

Charity didn't worry that she'd woken him from his beauty sleep. The man could turn himself on and off like a robot. He answered, so he was on.

"I need help, Colonel," she replied, unfussed by his rudeness. It was what made the man who he was. "I'm in Campeche, Mexico and the daughter of a U.S. federal judge was kidnapped from here less than an hour ago, while vacationing with her mother. I am on the judge's chartered boat now with the mother."

There was a long pause.

"Harper Landry?"

"How did—"

"We already have assets headed to your location," he interrupted. "I didn't bother contacting you, since I knew you were already there."

She glanced over at the captain, who was talking to Suzette.

"Did the captain call you?" she asked. "Who are you sending?"

"I don't know anything about any captain," Stockwell grumbled. "One of our assets heard a Mayday and is headed toward your location now. She contacted Livingston, who called me to see if we had anyone nearby."

"Savannah McDermitt?" Charity asked, hoping she was both right and wrong at the same time.

"She'll arrive there by boat at dawn to coordinate logistics," Stockwell replied. "Savannah will be in charge, while you go pick up Bender and Martin at Campeche International at oh-eight-hundred and begin the investigation. I expect individual reports from each of you no later than ten hundred hours, and Savannah will give me hourly updates after that."

DJ Martin? Charity thought, a mix of regret and anticipation

93

coursing through her veins. But before she could say anything, the call went dead.

She looked up from her phone to see everyone staring at her. "What's wrong?" the captain asked.

Charity quickly gathered her senses. "Nothing. I was just checking with my superiors, and we have help coming."

"Yes, I know," Suzette said. "Savannah texted me and told me who you were."

Oh shit....

"What exactly did Savannah say?" Charity asked. "In the text, I mean."

Suzette held her phone up and looked at it, swiping her finger and tapping the screen.

"The first one was an hour ago; she said she heard the Mayday and was returning." She paused and looked up at Charity. "The second one I just received a few minutes ago, telling me you were both investigators and said I could trust you. She also said she is bringing friends, and to tell *you* not to go anywhere."

They'd divided up the watches into one-hour segments, and Charity had taken the three o'clock mid-watch. After a few hours of sleep, she'd relieved Karina, and had spent the last hour in *MollySue's* galley, perched on a stool, using her phone and the yacht's internet to look up anything she could on Harper's father. She had Suzette's phone on the counter beside her, plugged into a charger.

Before taking a sedative and going to bed, Suzette had called her husband again, telling him to text her when he heard anything, and that someone would be monitoring her phone all night.

The kidnappers still haven't called, Charity thought.

Of course, if a demand *was* made, it would likely be to the judge himself. It just didn't sit right with Charity that he wasn't on the next plane after learning his daughter had been abducted and a man murdered.

Stockwell's words kept coming back to Charity's mind. He'd made it a point to tell her that Savannah was in charge. Charity was *always* on his shit list, so she'd assumed this was just more of the same.

But a civilian?

Charity wasn't the only one on Colonel Stockwell's shit list. There were a few other operatives on it, as well, like DJ Martin.

But telling her that Savannah was running this operation? A virtual neophyte? When both she and DJ had far more experience?

Even Bender would have been a more logical choice. And the psychologist wasn't on Stockwell's shit list. Not that she knew of.

Charity and DJ had had a little fling once—it was nothing—and they'd both agreed it'd been a mistake the next morning. A very enjoyable mistake, but one they decided was probably best not to repeat.

But there was no way Stockwell could have known about that. She and DJ were professionals. They would work together on this without a problem.

But putting Savannah in charge? What was that all about? Maybe it was just Stockwell's way of keeping her and the boy out of harm's way, while at the same time, surrounding her with assets that could exfiltrate her and Alberto quickly. With Savannah working behind the scenes as she'd done the night Paladin and Cordova were killed, he could more easily keep tabs on her.

So be it, Charity thought, tapping and reading another feel-good headline about Judge Jean Landry.

Charity had worked under others before, and she'd do it this time. The important thing was getting the girl back safely.

After that, with her search for Savannah finally over, Charity would have to talk to her about what happened. She hadn't planned for it to be under these circumstances, but it would happen just the same.

She tapped another story and scanned it.

And just why was Stockwell sending Paul Bender?

Besides being a very capable covert operative and former agent for the Secret Service, Paul was also a forensic psychologist, specializing in the study of the criminal mind.

A shrink, all the same.

She guessed it made sense to have him available for the victim and the mother, as well as for negotiating with the kidnappers.

Or did Deuce's or Stockwell's reason for sending him have more to do with *her* than it did the victims?

Charity often thought the people around her had ulterior motives, and occasionally they did. Jesse had once summed it up quite well when he once said that just because you're paranoid doesn't mean that *nobody* is out to get you.

She pushed those thoughts aside and opened yet another article about the Landrys.

Everything she'd found on Judge Jean Landry pointed to him being exactly what his wife described.

They lived in a modest home in a middle-income neighborhood on the outskirts of New Orleans.

Both drove older vehicles that had been bought used.

They were active in many community organizations, to which they donated a lot of money.

Their daughter went to an in-state college and the tuition was paid each semester, always on time.

Charity found not one single reference to the judge being dirty. Not even a hint at it.

Harald snored, then rolled over.

Suzette and the crew were asleep in cabins below deck, but the Dutch couple and the young videographers were sacked out across the counter from her in the spacious salon.

A soft beeping came from where the younger couple was slumped together on the couch. Trevor woke and touched his watch, then gently slid out from beside his wife, covering her with the light blanket they'd shared.

He held up a finger, mouthed the words "be right back," then disappeared down the stairs, Charity assumed, to the bathroom.

When he returned a moment later, his once disheveled hair was neatly combed.

"No call, huh?" he whispered.

Charity shook her head. "I'm beginning to think this whole thing isn't about money."

"What else, then?" Trevor asked.

"I don't know," Charity replied, slipping out from behind the counter and handing Suzette's phone to Trevor. She nodded toward the Dutch couple. "I'm going to sleep outside. Harald snores."

Charity picked up the blanket she'd been sitting on from the stool and quietly opened the large, sliding glass door.

The interior was illuminated by reduced red lighting, so her eyes were already mostly accustomed to the dark.

MollySue's stern faced west, and she could see the vast expanse of the Milky Way all the way down to the horizon, the stars only slightly washed out by the setting full moon.

She lay down on a recliner, pulled the blanket over her, and was soon fast asleep.

CHAPTER ELEVEN

As Charity lay sleeping, her subconscious began to drift and her breathing became as labored as it had the night she and Jesse had finished their hard swim back to his boat.

"You need to let the others know what happened," Charity heard her own voice saying, the words echoing in her subconscious mind. In a dream state, she looked quickly all around. She and Jesse were safely back aboard his boat. "They're probably worried."

Jesse looked past her. "Police boat. Let's get inside."

Opening one of the fish boxes in the deck, they quickly shoved and kicked the dive gear into it, then went into the salon.

Jesse dug his comm out of his dry bag and put it in his ear. "Sitrep!"

Charity did the same.

"We started getting a lot of activity on local police communications," Chyrel said, as Jesse powered up his laptop. "Are y'all okay?"

"We're fine," he replied, sitting in front of the laptop.

In seconds, the machine connected with the encrypted Armstrong satellite and Chyrel and Chip appeared on the screen in the upper two corners.

A satellite view of Jesse's boat was at the bottom left, and a scrolling wall of text was in the other corner.

"We have the RBPF communications, Jesse," Chyrel said, looking up at her camera. "The computer is transcribing verbal radio communication in real time. They're reporting a shooting. What happened?"

"Didn't you see?" he asked, leaning close to the screen to read the police radio chatter.

He glanced over at Charity, then continued to read.

"The satellite's still too far away to see the beach," Savannah replied, though her image wasn't on the screen.

"When we started getting reports of gunshots," Chip added, "I trained the satellite on your boat, and we saw you go aboard."

"What happened, Jesse?" Savannah asked.

Charity noted a touch of anger in her friend's voice.

"They were at the bar, watching *Mer-Sea* at the dock," Jesse explained. "We got the drop on them and were able to get them to leave, but a waitress ran after us."

"Paladin used the distraction to go on the offensive," Charity said, leaning close to Jesse, letting her hair drip water onto his shoulder.

"He's dead," Jesse said flatly. "Both of them are."

"You shot them both?" Savannah asked, clearly upset.

"No," he replied. "Paladin managed to land a kick to my gun hand when the girl yelled. It went off before I dropped it."

"Then who got shot?" Chyrel asked.

"Nobody," Charity replied. "The Bahamian police will probably think the two murders were gang- or drug-related."

"They're mounting a search," Chyrel said. "On land *and* on the water."

"You said you would bring them in to stand trial," Savannah

said, her voice low. "He was someone we knew. Someone Alberto had looked up to."

"They didn't leave us any—"

"That's BS and you know it," Savannah spat in apparent outrage, becoming emotional. "Both of you... Either one of you could have..." There was silence for a moment. "Those men didn't have to die."

"You weren't there," Jesse stated, his voice sounding cold and on the verge of anger. "How close are the police boats?"

"Um... yeah," Chip stuttered. "There are two of them, each heading to two other boats in the anchorage you're in. Yours is the only other boat."

Jesse got up and grabbed Charity's bag from the salon. "Go get changed. They'll be here in a few minutes."

Then he turned to look at the computer. "We'll discuss the rest of this later. Right now, I don't think it'd be a good idea to go tearing out of here."

"The first police boat is at a sailboat," Chip said. "One guy's covering it with a machine gun or something, while the other is pounding on the hull."

"We're going silent again," Jesse said, closing the laptop, and pushing Charity down the companionway.

"Change in there," he said, steering her toward the guest cabin, before going on to the forward stateroom.

Charity put her bag on one of the two small beds and opened it. The door was open, and she could hear Jesse pulling drawers open in his cabin.

After peeling the dive skin off, she opened a couple of drawers and found a small stack of towels in the hanging locker next to a robe with the *Gaspar's Revenge* logo on the breast and Savannah's name under it.

She quickly towel-dried her hair, pulled her bikini bottom off, and put on a clean pair of panties from her go-bag.

The sound of a powerful outboard drew closer as Jesse raced past the open door wearing a bathrobe.

"They're here," he said needlessly.

"Stall them," Charity shouted. "Tell them we're a married couple on our honeymoon or something innocent like that. Just don't piss them off."

A spotlight passed over the small porthole as Charity began digging through her bag to find something to put on. She stopped as she pulled out a pair of high-waisted capri pants.

Jesse had been wearing a bathrobe.

"Dis is de police!" a man's voice shouted, as he banged on the hull. "Come out of dere now!"

Charity thrust the pants back into the bag and returned to the hanging locker. She grabbed the robe, then hurried out of the cabin and up to the galley, where she could see Jesse standing in the fully illuminated cockpit.

"Here now!" he shouted indignantly. "What's going on out here?"

"I am Sergeant Grant wit' de Royal Bahamas Police Force," the man said. "Who are you? And are you alone?"

"Name's McDermitt," Jesse replied. "Captain Jesse McDermitt from Florida. No, I'm not alone. My wife and I just arrived in the Bahamas an hour ago, and we're waiting to clear customs in the morning. We just got married."

Charity grinned and moved toward the door.

"You are wet," the cop said, suspicion in his voice.

"Of course he is," Charity said, stepping out into the bright lights behind Jesse. "We were in the shower."

The spotlight moved unsteadily, and whoever was holding it gasped.

Jesse turned and his eyes became as wide as saucers, but he quickly recovered.

The lead policeman turned his back, but only for a second. "Turn off dat light!" he ordered the second man. "And Ms. McDermitt, please make yuhself decent."

"That's twice in one day," Charity mumbled, pulling the robe on. "I don't know if my fragile ego can handle this lack of attention."

"What's the meaning of all this?" Jesse pushed, sounding every bit the indignant aristocrat as he took a step toward the gunwale and pointed to the top of the outrigger. "We have the proper quarantine flag displayed. Customs isn't open until morning. We're anchored conspicuously and properly with the anchor light on. We've done nothing to warrant this kind of intrusion."

The cop looked back, saw that she'd covered herself, then turned to face Jesse. "Dere were gunshots on de beach not fifteen minutes ago," he said. "You had to hear dem."

Charity covered her mouth, pretending to be embarrassed. "We've, um... well, we've been in bed the last hour."

"De shots didn't wake you?" Grant asked.

"I didn't say we were asleep," she replied, moving closer to Jesse. "We were... uh... preoccupied."

"Yes... well... okay," the cop stammered. "And you've seen and heard nothing since you arrived?"

Jesse looked at her and grinned, then turned his attention back to the policeman. "I think we've all seen enough."

"Yes, well, keep a watch," the cop said, pushing their boat away. "Dere was two murduhs tonight."

The police left, heading toward the trawler where the other police boat was, and Charity went inside with Jesse, who switched off the outside lights, plunging them into near total darkness again.

Jesse watched the boats carefully through the side glass. Charity joined him in the galley, also watching.

"I think we're in the clear," she offered.

"What was the idea, coming out there naked like that?"

"I wasn't naked," she said. "You use a ghillie suit to disguise your actions—I use whatever I have available. It worked."

"Let's get dressed and get out of here," he said, heading toward the sleeping quarters.

"We can't," she said, staring at all the lights. "If we leave now, it'll look suspicious."

"So, we just hang around here all night?"

Her vision had adjusted to the darkened interior, so she stepped past him and went down the steps, letting the robe slip down over her shoulders, then turning and giving Jesse a coy smile. "Oh, I can think of a thing or two to pass the time."

He rolled his eyes as she turned into the guest stateroom, leaving the door open. Jesse went past her into his cabin, and she heard the door close.

Charity knew she wasn't going to be able to sleep after what had happened. So, she decided to take the cops' warning. She pulled the robe back on, got her earwig from her dry bag, and left the small guest cabin.

She quietly closed the door, glancing for a moment at Jesse's, then slipped silently up to the flybridge in bare feet.

Opening the overhead panel, Charity found the box and put the miniature device back where it belonged before walking around the helm and sitting on the forward-facing bench in front of it.

She looked up at the night sky. The moon was behind them, almost to the western horizon, so she could clearly see thousands of stars to the east.

The police boats were gone, and one light from the trawler's aft stateroom still shone, but after a few more minutes, it too went off and Charity was alone with her thoughts.

The night was hot and muggy, and the bathrobe thick, so she loosened the sash and let it fall back over her shoulders. The cool breeze off the water tickled and cooled her skin.

A moment later, she heard the click of the salon door closing, then footsteps on the ladder.

"That was crazy, huh?" she whispered without turning.

"I thought you'd gone to bed," Jesse said from behind her.

Charity heard him opening one of the cabinets and rummaging around. She didn't answer right away, as Jesse sat at the helm and typed something on his phone.

"Poor timing on the waitress's part," Charity finally said, her voice quiet as she stared up at the stars. "It was all the distraction Paladin needed."

She regretted saying it as soon as the words came out. Jesse was a proud man. But he was also moving up in years and his reaction time *had* been slow.

"Say what's on your mind," he said, his tone even.

She turned slightly and faced him. She couldn't see his face clearly; the moon was just over his left ear, silhouetting his face and broad shoulders.

She sighed. Now wasn't the time.

"You're slowing down, Jesse," she said softly. "You know it, and tonight that microsecond almost got us both killed."

"I didn't hear your gun go off," he said defensively.

"I turned to shoot Paladin when I saw what was going to happen," she explained, keeping her voice soft. "Cordova was fast. Faster than I would have thought. He tackled me before I could get a shot off."

She didn't want to tell him that if he'd not been distracted and had fired when Paladin made his move, her own gun would have taken out Cordova, as well. It was that microsecond of hesitation that had caused them to have to fight for their lives.

"Could we both be getting too old?" he grumbled.

She sensed a bit of humor in his tone and smiled.

"Ha! Speak for yourself, jarhead."

He just stood there, then turned his head toward the sky ahead of them, as if he'd seen something.

"You know," she said with a soft sigh, "there may be some truth in that." She paused, wondering how open she should be. "I sometimes feel like I'm getting slow. However, when you and I work together, I'd say we're damned near invincible."

His face came up, though she couldn't see it. "We should get some sleep," he said, heading over to the ladder. "I told Savannah I'd give her a call when we hoist anchor."

"You go ahead," she said, turning to catch a meteor streaking through the sky. "I'm just going to sit here a while."

"G'night, then," he said, then went down the ladder.

A few minutes later, she saw the hatch in the foredeck open to catch the cool breeze, and Charity was again alone with her thoughts.

She could have stepped out into the bright lights fully clothed, but with him in a robe and telling the cops they were newlyweds, that would have appeared odd, if not suspicious. And what she'd done had the immediate effect she'd wanted—the cops had left them alone.

She stood, letting the bathrobe fall to the deck, and stepped up to the rail. She thought of Victor, and how much she missed him.

Just as a tear rolled down her cheek, she heard the heavy creak of the steps and looked over her shoulder to see Jesse coming back up.

Charity turned to face him. He was once more silhouetted against the moon so that his features were inscrutable. She stood in the shadow of the roof, the moonlight only reaching her knees.

Charity took a step toward him, out of the shadow, exposing herself.

He made a move toward her, then they rushed into one another's arms, kissing and caressing each other.

Charity felt a passion she'd never felt before as she ran her fingers under Jesse's shirt, feeling the slabs of muscle on his chest, then pushing his shirt up and over his head.

CHAPTER TWELVE

Charity twisted and squirmed on the deck lounger, then woke suddenly, sitting straight up with her eyes squeezed tightly shut. She slammed both fists into the cushion. "Stop it, damn you! Just stop!"

Hands grabbed her shoulders. "Charity! Wake up!"

Her eyes flew open, locking onto Savannah's face as she drew back her right fist, ready to strike.

Charity blinked. *Savannah?*

She was there—right in front of her.

For an instant, Charity's eyes started to well up, then Savannah pulled her into a tight hug.

"It's okay," Savannah whispered. "It was just a bad dream. You're safe now. Nobody will hurt you."

Savannah? Here, already?

Charity blinked her eyes again and saw that it was daylight—still early morning, but she'd been asleep at least two hours. Savannah must have thought she was having a nightmare.

"I'm okay," she stammered uncomfortably, pushing Savannah away. "I can't believe it's you. That I've found you."

Savannah shoved herself backward and her blue eyes turned cold. "I told him explicitly not to come after me *or send anyone!*"

Charity suddenly remembered the letter Jesse had told her about. "He didn't send me," she said, rising from the deck recliner. "I came on my own. He doesn't even know I've been looking for you, but I have been ever since you left. It wasn't—"

"I don't care!" Savannah hissed, then looked back over to the other side of the cockpit, where the captain stood nervously, looking at them. "We have more important things to do." Savannah paused and took a deep breath. "Our past," she continued, quickly pointing her finger back and forth between them, "*and* our future, are on hold. There's a lot of work to be done."

This was a different Savannah, Charity thought. She hadn't noticed it over the years, but she seemed more sure of herself, more decisive.

"Stockwell said Bender and Martin were arriving at oh-eight-hundred," Charity said, looking at her watch.

"He texted me ten minutes before we anchored," Savannah said, nodding toward her trawler, anchored less than a hundred feet away. "There's supposed to be a car and driver waiting for you at the pier. Are you sure you're okay?"

Charity wasn't used to being an underling, but Savannah had been her friend once, and maybe could be again.

But dreaming about your friend's husband? Then the friend waking you from that dream? Charity's hands were still shaking.

"Yeah. Fine... I guess I... um... better get going."

Halfway down the steps, Savannah called out, "And Charity?"

She stopped and turned around slowly, ready for whatever wrath Savannah would unleash on her.

"Circumstances aside," Savannah said, then smiled, "it really is very nice to see you."

Then she turned to the captain. "I'll need digital access to your most powerful radio."

Charity continued down the steps, bewildered by Savannah's heartfelt comment.

Nice to see me again? she thought. Who in their right mind could be happy to see the person who'd broken up their marriage?

Then she caught herself. Of course she'd say that to cover up the tension they'd created.

Her heart rate was still elevated when she stepped down into her dinghy and started the engine. One moment she'd been with Savannah's husband in her dream, and the next Savannah was right in front of her,

She shook her head, trying to shake off the uncomfortable scene, untied the line, and started to push away.

"Charity!" Savannah called down.

She held onto the swim platform and looked up.

"Drop DJ off in town," Savannah said. "He has the address. He's to meet a local woman who might have some information."

"Got it," she called back up, as casually as she could. She wouldn't let anyone suspect she was shaken by Savannah's attitude.

She didn't really mind Stockwell putting Savannah in charge; that kind of thing happened all the time—the handler had the overall big picture, being in touch with all the moving parts. And it kept her and Alberto safe.

She wondered for a moment, as she idled away, where the boy was. She'd probably sent him down below. The younger crewman was only a couple of years older than Alberto.

Twisting the throttle, Charity brought the dinghy up to planing speed and steered toward the main port of entry dock, which extended out over half a mile from the city's waterfront.

When she arrived, Charity tied her dinghy at the designated

spot near the foot of the long pier and climbed up a ladder right next to the guard's gate.

She smiled at the guard, handing him her passport, already open to the current entry stamp, and he quickly waved her through.

A minivan was idling at the curb, and as she approached it, the driver's door opened and a young man stepped out and smiled at her.

"Senorita Ortiz-Fleming?" he asked, smiling.

"*Si,*" Charity replied, a bit surprised. He was at least ten years younger but had used the term for a young single woman. "*Eres mi coche al aeropuerto?*"

He replied that yes, he was her ride to the airport and opened the back door for her. Charity went past him, opting for the front passenger seat.

"*Hablas inglés?*" she asked, sliding into the front seat.

"Yes," he replied. "I speak very good English. You?"

She laughed. "I'm American," she replied. "From California."

"Ah, I see," he said, putting the car into gear. "Your Spanish is excellent."

"But a bit stilted?"

He grinned over at her. "I went to university in Mexico City," he said, turning into a traffic circle. "I had an English teacher who was from Seville and she spoke exactly the same way."

Charity doubted it was exact. She spoke Spanish with a Cuban flair, which was close to the Castilian Spanish of Spain, but not quite. She would have to work on her Mexican dialect.

When they arrived at the airport, she spotted DJ immediately, both by his shaggy hair and goatee, and by the fact that he was wearing cargo shorts, exposing the sticker-covered prosthetic he wore in place of his lower right leg.

The first night they'd spent together in Pensacola, DJ had shared with her how he'd lost his foot in Iraq, and she'd shared her experience of crashing and losing the men she'd been charged with evacuating from the battlefield.

"Pull over there," Charity told the driver. "The guy with the peg leg."

The driver, who'd introduced himself as Enrique, grinned. "Missing leg or not, he looks like a very capable man."

Enrique was right. As the car approached the two men, Charity couldn't help but notice that DJ had slimmed down even more since they'd last seen each other.

Had it been over a year since she'd sent him on his way, back in Apalachicola?

Just as she started to open the window, he spotted her and smiled. She felt the heat rise in her cheeks.

"Get in," she told them when the car stopped.

Bender went around and got in behind the driver as DJ dropped into the seat behind her. Both men carried only shoulder bags.

As Charity started to turn to face them, she felt a pull on the back of her seat and suddenly DJ's face was right in hers.

"So, uh, what's goin' on?" he asked, one corner of his mouth turning up in what would be a boyish grin if it weren't for all the hair.

She stared into his eyes for a moment, then snapped out of it. "You know more than me. Who's this person we're dropping you off to talk to?"

DJ cocked his head toward the driver. "Eak-spay english-nay?"

She couldn't help herself and smiled. "Yes, this is our driver, Enrique. And he speaks better English than you do pig latin."

"Hey, Enrique," DJ said. "Pleased to meet ya. I'm Bob McKenzie and this is my brother, Doug. He don't talk much."

Bender gave her a wink. "Take off, hoser."

"I wonder if it'd be too much trouble to ask you to step out of the car for just a minute?" DJ asked, smiling at Enrique. "We have somethin' private to discuss before we go anywhere."

"Um, sure," Enrique said, shutting off the engine.

"Leave the motor runnin', compadre," DJ said. "It's Africa-hot out there."

Charity touched Enrique's arm. "It's okay."

He glanced back at the two men, then restarted the engine and climbed out.

"All I was told was to drop you off somewhere," Charity said. "Did she learn something already?"

"How *you* doin'?" DJ said, smiling. "You don't text. You don't call."

"Focus, DJ. It's good to see you both again."

"Likewise," Bender said, staring out the window.

"All I know is a woman named Rosita Gonzales will be at a place called the *Coco Bongo*," DJ replied, accenting the name as if he enjoyed saying it. "She's a CI, supposed to know somethin' about the kidnappers. I thought you were in charge."

"No, Stockwell put Savannah in charge."

Bender turned to face her. "Savannah McDermitt?" he asked, surprise evident in his usually stoic voice.

"Savvy's here?" DJ asked, grabbing her seat back and pulling himself forward again.

"You two didn't know?"

"I heard she'd disappeared," DJ said, "but since then, everyone's been absolutely hush-hush about anything else. He's a real private guy and I really only know him through Armstrong. Not somethin' ya call a guy ya barely know and ask about."

"Yeah, well, she's here," Charity said. "She'll be acting as handler on the investigation. Who told you to contact this woman?"

"That came from Deuce," Bender responded.

"Chyrel's working on it," Charity said, thinking out loud. "Where did you fly in from? Bimini?"

"Aw, hell no," DJ replied. "I was visitin' my cousin and some friends up in Homosassa, Florida, supposedly on R and R."

"Did your partner get a new boat yet?" Charity asked, just making conversation as she plugged more information into what was going on. *Pulling someone from vacation?*

"Jerry?" DJ scoffed. "It took him two years to decide on *Wayward*. Naw, he's still lookin'."

"I was more than happy to get out of Fort Meade," Bender said. "They call it the Puzzle Palace for a very good reason."

"What were you doing there?" she asked, truly curious.

"Giving a series of lectures on the criminal mind as it might relate to foreign heads of state or dictators."

Charity shook her head. "With Russian oligarchs disappearing left and right, I can't believe nobody's taken their places who has balls enough to take him out."

"Putin?" DJ chuckled. "They're too busy avoiding bridges and balconies."

"The GRU used to be fairly covert about it," Paul said. "Now, they just shoot them or push them in front of a train."

Vacation aside, sending someone from Florida, Charity could understand. But would Paul Bender in Maryland be the next closest asset?

Charity tapped the horn and Enrique got back in.

"We're going back to the pier," she told him. "Do you know

WAYNE STINNETT AND KIMBERLI A. BINDSCHATEL

where Coco Bongo is?"

"Oh, yes," he replied, putting the car in gear. "Is a very nice place. Good food."

"Stop there on the way. We'll be dropping one of my friends off."

Ten minutes later, the car pulled to the curb across from an open-air cantina with steel bars for window screens.

"That's it?" DJ asked, looking across the street. "The rusty red building?"

"Yes," Enrique replied. "It may not look like much from the outside, but is much larger inside."

Just as DJ got out, a woman in a red dress with black trim stepped out of the cantina, looked up and down the street, then waved as DJ stood up. She had thick, jet-black hair, long and wavy, with a red poinsettia over one ear.

She only needs a flamenco guitar in her hands to complete the ensemble, Charity thought.

DJ stuck his head back in and grinned. "Don't wait up for me."

CHAPTER THIRTEEN

When Charity and Paul got back to the *MollySue*, introductions were made and then Bender went inside to the large dinette with Suzette and the captain.

Charity could tell that the psychologist had a lot of questions for Savannah. She also knew he wouldn't ask a single one of them.

Savannah told Charity that while she was picking up the two men, the coroner had arrived on another police boat to take the body of the dead crewman to the morgue, and Trevor had shown her the card the policeman who was with the coroner had given everyone. His name was Sergeant Ra'l Quintero.

"Up a rank from the other two, right?" he asked.

"But still just a sergeant," Charity said. "Unless the local commissioner or police chief gets involved, the cops will be of no help."

"We need to talk," Savannah said, taking Charity's elbow and turning her toward the stern.

Charity glanced over to the flybridge ladder and Savannah led the way. The two sat facing one another on a curved sofa in the shade of the flybridge's large bimini.

The wind at Savannah's back pushed her hair into her face. She tossed it over one shoulder and held it with her left hand.

Charity took a deep breath. "Look, I know what you must have—"

"Do you sense something wrong about this kidnapping?" Savannah interrupted.

"Wrong?"

How could she stay so focused when the woman who'd caused her and Jesse to split up was right across the table from her?

She'd never thought Savannah could be so composed, so able to compartmentalize. It was impressive, actually.

"What do you mean?" Charity asked.

Savannah looked at her phone. "It's been almost twelve hours since Harper was taken."

"And no ransom demand," Charity said.

"So, you think that's weird, too?"

"More than a little," Charity replied.

"Do you think the judge might be in on it?"

Charity sat back. "The judge? Kidnapping his own daughter? What for?"

"He's not here," Savannah said. "Why isn't he here?"

"I don't think he's involved," Charity said. "I dug into his background last night." She shook her head slowly. "But I don't think it's a kidnapping for ransom either."

"What else, then?"

Charity shrugged. "That'd be a question for Bender. Blackmail, maybe?"

"He's a judge," Savannah stated, ticking off an imaginary number one on her finger. "His daughter's kidnapped. He doesn't come to where it happened. And according to his wife, he has a very important case on his docket."

Four boxes ticked.

"You think whatever this case is that he can't get away from might have something to do with Harper being taken?" Charity asked, already thinking it herself.

"That would make his not being here make sense," Savannah replied. "What did you find out about him?"

"So clean, he radiates," Charity replied. "From what I learned about the man, if it is blackmail, and if the kidnappers grabbed Harper to force him to decide a certain way on a certain case, Judge Jean Landry would have a serious battle with his own conscience."

"That straight?" Savannah asked. "He'd risk his daughter's safety in the name of justice?"

"He strikes me as a bit of a zealot," Charity replied. "He might."

"That raises the stakes considerably," Savannah said, nodding.

"No kidding," Charity agreed. "How blind can justice be?"

"Water taxi headed this way," Paul Bender shouted from below.

The two women went quickly down the steps to find Paul looking toward the pier with a pair of binoculars.

He handed them to Charity and pointed toward a boat approaching the *MollySue* from the east.

"Besides the driver," Paul commented, shading his eyes, "looks like three other people aboard."

"I'm going in to check on Suzette," Savannah said. "And I want to talk to the captain again, and the crewman who saw one of the abductors." She pointed at the approaching boat. "Unless they have information, get rid of them."

As Savannah disappeared inside, Charity and Paul looked at one another, then at Savannah retreating into the salon and closing the door. Paul shrugged and Charity raised the binoculars to assess who was headed their way.

Stockwell had made it clear that Savannah was calling the shots.

If she didn't want to find out what these people wanted, that was fine with Charity.

"What the?" she muttered.

"What is it?" Paul asked.

"One of them, I believe, is a man I met just over a year ago up in the Florida panhandle. Name's Jyotiraditya Laghari, or Jojo. He's an investment broker and a devotee of tantric meditation. I thought then that he was a very mysterious guy. I liked him but couldn't quite figure him out."

She lowered the binos for a moment and looked over at Paul. "Suzette said her husband was sending his financial guy. Maybe it's him. Though that'd be quite a coincidence."

"I don't know," Paul said, as Charity put the binos back up to her eyes. "New Orleans isn't far from there."

"How often do separate coincidences collide?" she asked, observing the red- haired woman with Jojo.

Paul moved a little closer, leaning on the bulkhead and watching her. "What do you mean?" he asked.

Charity was uncomfortable under the man's gaze, but since she held the only pair of binoculars, what else was he supposed to look at?

"Well, the redhead on the left looks a lot like a young woman I met in The Bahamas just before Jesse, Deuce, and I joined Armstrong." She paused as the woman said something to the second man. "Yes, I'm sure it's her, with that perky nose and wild red hair. I believe her name is *Poppy*."

"You don't sound as if you thought much of this woman," Paul commented, letting the statement hang.

Charity lowered the binoculars to look at him. "You came to that conclusion from what? My tone of voice?"

Paul shrugged, arching an eyebrow as if to say, "It's what I do."

"It's not that exactly," she replied, a little annoyed that he seemed to be able to read her thoughts. "She seemed capable enough, I guess. Just a bit unorthodox, if you ask me. If my memory serves, she's with Fish and Wildlife."

"Fish and Wildlife?" Paul said, turning his head once more to look at the approaching boat. "And a meditating financial broker. Odd."

"A bit of an understatement, in my opinion," Charity said, raising the binoculars again. "Especially considering the source. I wouldn't have thought you guys saw anything as 'odd.'"

"Just an expression."

"I don't recognize the third person, but he seems to be there with her and not Jojo. Not sure what brings them our way."

"Well, there's one way to find out." Paul turned and headed for the stern to greet them.

The taxi pulled up alongside the swim platform and the three passengers stepped aboard the *MollySue*.

Charity's presumption was confirmed—it was definitely Jojo and Poppy.

"Ah," Jojo said, opening his arms in a big gesture of hello, smiling broadly at her. "We meet again."

Charity stepped toward him, thrusting her hand forward. "Jojo, right? How is your friend, The Buddha?"

Poppy gave her a curious look, but Jojo seemed to understand that Charity didn't want the others knowing the depth of their friendship. It wasn't that they had anything to hide, it was just her way— she preferred to separate acquaintances from coworkers.

"Yes, Jojo Laghari," he replied, shaking her hand. "The Buddha is serene, as usual. I'll tell him you asked. But much more pressing, I represent the Landrys' interests, and that is why I am here."

He turned to acknowledge his companions. "And this is Poppy McVie, an agent with Fish and Wildlife."

Charity was sure the young woman recognized her, but said nothing. Nobody needed to know that they'd sort of met once before.

Had she misjudged the Fish and Wildlife agent back then? Could she be working undercover now?

When they'd first met, Poppy had seemed like a loose cannon to her. Jesse had liked her, taken her under his wing, helped her on a case she'd been working, which Charity didn't think he should have gotten so involved with.

Now she wondered, had she been jealous? Poppy was young and sexy and, as far as she could tell, pretty bright. So of course Jesse would've been drawn to her.

"And Kevin Ferris," Jojo continued, "who is with a, uh... an independent investigative service."

Charity stepped forward and shook both their hands. "Charity Styles, Homeland Security." She gestured toward Paul. "Paul Bender, forensic psychologist with Armstrong Research and former Secret Service agent."

"Woowee," Kevin said, his hands landing on his hips theatrically. "Aren't we in some fine company. This is getting more and more interesting by the minute." He turned to Jojo. "Did you know there was already a team in place?"

Jojo shook his head.

"Well, I suppose a debrief is in order right away."

"Indeed," Charity said. Her gaze moved to Poppy. "Let's start with why Fish and Wildlife is involved in a kidnapping."

"I think we should start with why *DHS* would be involved," Kevin said. "Yeah, Judge Landry's a federal judge, but presides over a small district court."

Jojo, with his warm, welcoming demeanor, held his hands out, smiling. "I am sure both will be interesting stories." He gestured toward the cockpit table, shaded by the overhanging rear part of the flybridge. "Shall we get out of the hot sun?"

CHAPTER FOURTEEN

The ad hoc group of investigators went up to the cockpit, where it was noticeably cooler. Paul and Poppy slid around the bench seat while Kevin and Charity sat next to them at either end of the U-shaped dinette. Jojo took the remaining deck chair and smiled at Charity.

Grudgingly, she turned to Kevin. "Friend of Suzette's," she said, not really lying very much. "I just happened to see the kidnapping go down from my own boat. The one at the end." She pointed to the far end of the anchorage, and as Poppy and Kevin turned to look, she added, "Besides being an agent for DHS, I'm also a contractor for Armstrong Research."

Poppy and Kevin both reacted to Armstrong's name, but said nothing.

"I contacted Kevin," Jojo began. "On Judge Landry's behalf, of course, as soon as he informed me of the ongoing investigation. I figured there must be some connection. It's all too much of a coincidence. Well, I'll let Kevin fill you in."

Kevin looked around at the group as he inched forward in his seat. "I work for WCEA—the Wildlife Crime Enforcement Alliance. We're a well-funded NGO that investigates wildlife crime globally, in tandem with agencies like U.S. Fish and Wildlife." He gestured toward Poppy, acknowledging her. "We generally gather intel, either by electronic means or undercover work, then turn it over to the authorities when there's enough for a warrant." He turned to Charity. "I believe this is similar to Armstrong's investigative branch."

Charity nodded, though she couldn't imagine their network being as vast as Jack Armstrong's, and it was doubtful their people were ever sent out to neutralize a specific target.

Kevin continued. "My team and I have been working on a case for over a year, trying to identify a notorious turtle exporter from the New Orleans area.

"The judge recently had a case pop up on his docket—the accused is a man by the name of Earl Hebert. Now, Earl's a two-bit criminal, recently arrested for catching and illegally selling endangered turtles. When he was booked, then released, we saw the opportunity to surveil him, see if we couldn't connect some dots. We figure he's selling to someone, right?"

Charity noticed Poppy shift uncomfortably, a slight pink flush to her cheeks.

"And you've connected Hebert to someone here in Mexico?" Charity asked.

Kevin shook his head. "No. We, uh...you see, Poppy and I met a few years ago, on another completely unrelated case. At the time, neither one of us realized the other was on the same side of the law. So, when we happened across each other in New Orleans, both looking for an exporter, well, we–"

Charity grinned. "You each suspected the other?"

Poppy finally spoke up. "Unfortunately, our supervisors didn't seem to think communication between our agencies was important. We'd been chasing each other, wasting time."

126

Kevin smirked. "I thought I'd bagged one helluva trophy."

Poppy's cheeks turned a darker shade of pink.

Charity glanced at Paul, whose expression was, as always, inscrutable to the average person. But Charity had been around enough shrinks to read through it, and she thought he might have come to the same conclusion as she had—these two had fallen for each other while playing cat and mouse. If you weren't careful, it happened— something Charity knew all too well.

Kevin's demeanor turned professional again. "As soon as we realized our mistake, we regrouped and compared notes. That's when JoJo called, saying the judge's daughter had been kidnapped here in Campeche. We don't know if it's connected or not, but these cartels often traffic in wildlife as well as drugs. The money is easy, with virtually no serious fines or penalties. We thought we'd hit the ground running, see if we could connect some more dots down here and help with the situation."

"You've yet to explain the connection," Paul said, his tone analytical. "Is there something in Mr. Hebert's background that you think directly ties him to *any* drug cartel, or to this area?"

"Not exactly. What we do know is that over the last year, U.S. Fish and Wildlife Service and U.S. Customs and Border Protection have intercepted Mexican box turtles illegally smuggled into the States. Guess where? You see, Mexican box turtles are a rare species, only found in eastern Mexico within the states of San Luis Potosi, Tamaulipas and Veracruz. That's just west of here.

"And trucking something to the northern Yucatan," Charity offered, "to go on a boat to the U.S. mainland, would drastically cut the distance the boat would have to travel. Much easier to smuggle something into a softer port like New Orleans, far from the Mexican border."

127

"That's not all," Kevin continued. "Customs also retrieved some that were shipped from New Orleans to China, packaged exactly the same way as the species good ol' Earl was selling. Coincidence? Maybe. We're here to find out. And, as I said, Poppy and I want to help get the judge's daughter back. Any way we can. Poppy happens to have some experience with cartel kidnapping."

"What kind of experience?" Charity asked.

"I was kidnapped," Poppy said, matter-of-factly.

Charity stared. "And?"

"Purposefully, I guess you could say. Trying to infiltrate..." She paused a moment.

"Coincidentally, they were also trafficking turtles," she added, as if she had just recalled that fact.

"Long story short, we busted a cartel boss." She glanced briefly at Kevin. "That was a while ago, though, and a long way from here. On the Pacific coast."

"The South Pacific Cartel has expanded east," Charity said. "Into northeast Mexico, and there have been reports of activity in some areas of the Yucatan. Logistically, it's much closer to the U.S. mainland if you're shipping by boat, and crossing a land border is always more difficult. It's very possible it's the same cartel that we're dealing with here."

Poppy nodded. "I'm not sure my experience would provide much help. My friend's fiancé had made some bad choices and brokered a deal with the cartel, then his plans went sour. I'm happy to provide details if you think it'll help, but it wasn't exactly your typical kidnapping-for-ransom situation. Though, I assume with the judge involved, that isn't what you've got here either."

"So far, we don't have much," Charity conceded, "and I have no idea if this ties into your case." She handed Poppy a sketch the young crewman had drawn.

"One of the perpetrators has a couple of distinctive tattoos. The facial features in this drawing aren't very good, but the crewman who saw him thinks he got the tats right. Does that match anyone in your purview?"

Poppy looked at the drawing, then handed the paper to Kevin. Both shook their heads.

"Tattoos like that aren't easy to hide," Kevin said.

"I don't think he tries to hide them," Charity replied.

Suzette came out of the salon and, when she saw Jojo, ran into his arms. "Oh, thank God you're here. Have they called? Do we know anything? What's the plan? I just don't understand any of this."

Savannah also came out and more introductions and explanations were made.

Charity's phone pinged an incoming text message from DJ. She read it and looked over at Savannah. "It's DJ," she said. "He wants us to come to where he is. There's more information that we should all hear."

"It's a good central location to start from," Savannah said. "After you find out what this woman knows, you can split up and start nosing around."

"Nosing around?" Charity asked.

"It's a Southern thing," she said with a wink. "A hound dog will trot with his nose to the ground when he's looking for something."

A wink? Charity thought. *If Savannah was acting chummy to avoid questions from the others, she was very good at it.*

"Come on, Paul," she said. "Let's get our noses to the ground."

"Mind if we tag along?" Poppy asked, stepping between Charity and the stairs to her dinghy.

"My dink's only big enough for two," Charity said, looking down at the smaller woman.

To her credit, Poppy didn't flinch or back down.

"Take the *MollySue's* tender," Savannah said, extending a float ring with a key. "The captain's given us full use of the yacht. There's another smaller tender if we need it."

"I'll drive," Paul said, taking the keys from Savannah,

Once the five of them went down to the swim platform, Paul pulled the tender up close so everyone could get aboard. Charity waited by the line until Paul got in and started the engine, then quickly untied the painter and stepped aboard.

"So," Poppy said, standing between Charity and Jojo, "you two... know each other, huh?"

Charity felt the heat rise in her cheeks. It wasn't what she'd asked, but the tone of her voice. She'd sensed something more between her and Jojo than a mere passing acquaintance and had immediately jumped to it being even more intimate than it was.

Charity smiled. "I used the services of an associate of Jojo's, a sound healer. Excuse me, but Paul and I have to send a report to our supervisor."

"The woman on the boat?"

"No, she's just our logistics handler," Charity replied. "We report to her boss."

Jojo's phone trilled in his pocket. He took it out and looked at it, then held up a finger to Charity.

"This is Judge Landry," he announced. "I must take the call."

Paul slowed the boat to reduce wind and engine noise and they all gathered around Jojo.

He answered the phone and listened for a moment, then said, "A meeting so soon?"

He listened another moment before asking the judge if he could

130

put him on speaker. "Jean, how it came about, I cannot explain," Jojo said. "But I am currently with a small army of agents from many American investigative agencies. Two of them are known personally to me. These are professionals, Jean. I am just a negotiator."

Finally, he tapped the screen, held the phone toward the middle of the group and said, "You're on the speaker, Jean." Then he looked up at Charity. "Jean has managed to arrange a meeting for me with the kidnappers."

"Not a good idea," she said, shaking her head. "It could be a trap. Judge Landry, my name's Charity Styles, and I work for DHS. Before that, I was a Miami cop. I just happened to be nearby when your daughter was taken. Did the kidnappers provide you with proof of life?"

"Proof of... well, no."

"I apologize for my partner's directness, sir," Paul said, in a soothing tone, leaning over Charity from the raised helm. "This is Paul Bender, also with Homeland Security. Sir, you should face this very real possibility and ask for proof that your daughter is still unharmed before entering negotiations."

"I will do that," he replied. "And I will send Jojo the details of the meeting."

"Is there a reason you're not here yourself?" Charity asked, again being blunt.

"I have... er, cases pending."

Charity leaned closer to Jojo's phone. "Does one of those cases involve the kidnappers, sir?"

"I am not at liberty to talk about *any* case currently before the court," he replied, in a way that told Charity he'd recited the same line a million times before.

She rolled her eyes and was about to say something when Jojo raised a finger and smiled.

"Jean, believe me. You can trust these people."

"I... can't take that chance, Jojo," the judge said with a heavy sigh.

There was silence, and then Jojo looked at his phone. "He has hung up."

The slow tender took ten minutes to reach the pier and there was another ten to get everyone through the customs checkpoint.

Several scenarios began to form in Charity's mind as to why the judge was physically missing.

And none of them were good.

CHAPTER FIFTEEN

It was brutally hot in the back of the cargo van. The odor was overwhelming—a mix of gasoline, manure, and sweat.

Harper struggled to breathe. It seemed like it'd been days since the attack on *MollySue*, but she felt certain only one night had passed. Maybe.

The men who'd dragged her off the yacht hadn't told her anything. She'd screamed, she'd cried, she'd gone limp. Nothing helped. Nothing mattered.

She'd been blindfolded and tied up as soon as they'd gotten her on the boat, and they didn't remove the blindfold until they'd reached shore and driven somewhere for at least ten or fifteen minutes.

Now she was in the back of the van again, once more blindfolded, but this time, they didn't seem to be taking her anywhere specific. It was like they'd just been driving in circles, stopping, then slowly moving, and stopping again. What was the point? To confuse her? She didn't even know which way the boat had taken her.

Why her? What was the reason for any of this?

Her mother had warned her to keep a vigilant awareness when they were in town. She'd always been smart, had been careful about keeping her eye on drinks at parties and had never walked home alone on campus.

In fact, her friends had teased her about her vigilance being over-the-top. Have a little fun, they'd told her. I do, she'd always replied.

Never think something couldn't happen to you. No matter where you are or the circumstance. Because she was an only child, Harper's parents had instilled this cautiousness in her from an early age.

Here in Mexico, when they were in town, or at the beach, she'd been hyper-vigilant. But on the boat, she thought she'd been safe.

She lifted both hands to wipe her nose, as they were tied together at the wrists. They hadn't given her much water or food, and the van felt as if it were spinning.

When will this be over?

After the previous night, when she could finally tell herself she was still alive and hadn't been raped, she mustered a sliver of calm to think.

She'd been kidnapped, that was clear. Maybe for ransom? It was the only thing that made sense. But why? Because she'd been on a big, fancy boat and had let her guard down?

Nothing else about this made any sense. Sure, her family was financially okay. Her dad *was* a judge, after all. But they weren't super wealthy. Not like some of the girls in her sorority, whose fathers could shell out a few million without batting an eye.

They could have had more, but her mom and dad were very philanthropic, donating time and money to many worthy causes. Harper had even worked with them, helping in a soup line several times.

Over the years, she knew her father had received the occasional death threat, usually from criminals he'd put in jail, but that was back home in Louisiana.

Her parents would be terrified, she knew, and her heart ached. If only she could call her mom.

She closed her eyes and tears came again. *I'm okay, Mom! I'm okay! I'm alive! Don't give up on me. Please!*

The van rolled to a stop. "*Aquí? El cabello, no?*"

The man in back with her moved, rocking the van. "*Es cabello rojo?*" he asked —the redhead?

"*Sí.*"

Harper understood Spanish the way it had been taught to her all through high school and college, but the Spanish these men spoke was fast and clipped, and seemed a guttural version of what she understood.

But she knew the words *caballo rojo* meant "red horse" and that's what they'd said.

The man in the back with her grabbed her under her armpits, lifted her, and dropped her in front of the sliding side door, pulling the blindfold off.

Harper blinked, unaccustomed to the bright sunlight.

"Don't move," the man ordered, the consequence if she disobeyed made perfectly clear by his tone.

Her eyes opened wide. It was the first time any of the men who'd taken her had said anything in English.

Don't move. Why? Were they going to get out of the van? Leave her alone? Could she get out? Maybe she could make a run for it.

She was sure they were still in Campeche. After they'd taken her to shore in the fishing boat, they'd transferred her to the van, then some shack that couldn't have been more than five miles away in her estimation.

Hours later, which felt like days, they'd forced her back into the van, but hadn't gone far, dragging her into another shack for a while. Then they'd brought her on this long, hot ride. Maybe the five miles back into town? She was sure the streets felt different, as though they'd gone from dirt roads to the paved and brick streets of the town.

She'd been allowed to remove the blindfold only two times while at the shack, and then only to go into the bathroom alone.

There'd been absolutely nothing in it she could have used as a weapon and there'd been no windows to escape through. There wasn't even a door.

During those few glimpses, she'd memorized the tattoos on her captor's neck. On his right side was an alligator, its teeth dripping blood. On the left was a snake, coiled to strike, its fangs longer than natural for any real snake she'd ever seen. The ink job looked like it'd been botched—probably done in the back room of some dive with a dirty needle.

She hoped, anyway.

He had an ugly scar on his chin, angling across the right side to the middle. *A knife cut?*

The driver grunted something to the tattooed man, and he repeated for her not to move, then flung open the sliding door behind her. She wanted to turn and look, see where she was, look for people, shout for help. But she didn't dare. She remained frozen as she'd been instructed.

But out of the corner of her eye, she saw a dark red building with steel bars over windowless openings. There were people moving. Still, Harper remained motionless.

The man pulled out a cell phone, snapped a picture out the door, then checked it was what he wanted before reaching over her shoulder for the handle and slamming the door shut again.

"*Vamos!*" he said to the driver, and the van lurched forward.

What was out the door? They seemed intent on getting to just the right spot. Why were they looking for a red horse? Was that her chance and she'd missed it? Now what? Would they kill her now?

Her gut clenched and her heart started to race out of control again. Would they take her back to the shack? What then?

Maybe the picture was for the ransom demand. She'd heard about that before. Something to prove she was still alive before the ransom was paid. Maybe if they took another picture, she could do... something. Send a signal. Anything.

The man glared at her, as if she were the reason he had that nasty scar on his chin.

She stared back, defiant. "Are you going to kill me now?"

He said nothing.

"I know you speak English. Tell me what's going on."

"*Callárse la boca!*" he snapped.

"Is this a Spanish lesson now?" she said through gritted teeth.

He glowered. "Shut up."

The van turned sharply around a corner and Harper lost her balance, flopping over on her side. The man shoved her back upright.

"If you've kidnapped me for ransom, you've made a mistake," Harper pleaded, her voice desperate. "I know that boat looks fancy, you know, big and expensive and all, but we don't own it. Just a rental. My dad saved for a long time for it. For a special trip, to celebrate, you know. We're not rich or anything."

He glowered again.

"I think you've got the wrong person," Harper implored. "I'm just a nobody. I'll just be starting my first job as a schoolteacher in another month."

His eyes fixed on her. "Shut up, Harper."

She drew in a breath as she sat bolt upright.

He knew her name. How'd he know her name?

The corners of his mouth moved slightly upward in a wicked grin.

Acid roiled in Harper's stomach. So she *was* the target. There was no mistake.

She leaned back against the van's door, her mind racing.

But why?

This had to be about her father. But he wouldn't be able to pay a big ransom. He'd put her through college and paid for this vacation to celebrate her graduation, which he'd then missed because he had to work. He funded the local food pantry and donated to the library. Her mother had always told her they didn't have a lot in savings and her father always feared money would corrupt, so he'd given it away as soon as it hit their bank account, except for what he and mom would need in retirement, and what she'd needed for college.

It was only because her mother had budgeted and planned on it since the day she'd learned she was pregnant with Harper that any of their income went to her education.

That was always a priority for her dad.

But that was it. No fancy cars, no big mansion, and summer vacations had been trips to the beach, somewhere along the Gulf Coast. Her parents had little savings that she knew of.

So when these kidnappers called her dad and he wasn't able to pay, what was going to happen?

The man with the tattoos stared at her, the grin still taunting her, as though he could read her thoughts.

At that moment, Harper knew she was as good as dead.

CHAPTER SIXTEEN

Enrique was again waiting at the foot of the pier and Charity introduced him to Poppy and Kevin.

None of them had said much of anything about the judge's short call, but it was at the top of Charity's mind, and she assumed the others were rolling his noncommittal statements around in their heads, too.

Halfway back to the cantina, Poppy finally broke the silence, voicing what Charity was thinking. She turned to Jojo. "Well, it goes without saying that Charity is right," she told him. "And we know why you and the judge can't say anything. But this silence doesn't help you get the girl back."

Charity touched Jojo's arm. "You not saying he's being blackmailed to rule on a case doesn't mean we don't all know it."

Jojo looked back and forth between the two women, then settled on Charity. "I have a... fiduciary responsibility to Judge Landry," he said quietly. "I cannot discuss this."

Enrique pulled to the curb in front of the restaurant and Paul was out of the front seat before the vehicle stopped, making a quick assessment of the area.

Charity got out and stood beside him, also scanning the area before the others climbed out.

"There they are," Paul said, nodding toward the second table along the left side of the interior of the elongated Coco Bongo cantina.

Charity ducked her head back inside the car. "Will you wait here for us, Enrique?"

He smiled. "I am at your disposal for as long as you need me."

Charity reached inside for her camera case, then decided it wasn't needed and left it.

Paul waited by the open doorway, scanning the street, as she led the others past him toward where DJ sat with his back to the wall, turned slightly toward the entrance, but still able to see the back.

Charity glanced that way and noticed a small stage, next to what appeared to be a back door at the far end of the dining area.

The dark-haired woman in the red dress Charity had seen earlier sat across from DJ, her back to them as they approached. To Charity's surprise, a guitar was propped on a third chair.

DJ spotted them coming and rose very quickly to his feet. "Jojo? What the hell are you doin' here, man? Did you bring The Buddha?"

Poppy gave Charity an odd look, no doubt curious after hearing The Buddha's name mentioned twice in an hour.

Paul brought up the rear, glanced quizzically at DJ, then he and Kevin pulled two tables together, and they all quickly arranged the chairs and sat down.

Charity sat next to DJ, facing the open-air front, and Paul sat at the opposite end, facing the back of the restaurant. Poppy and Kevin sat across from Jojo and the informant.

Jojo introduced DJ to everyone and, in a low voice, explained to him what his acquaintances' suspicions were and why he was there.

"This here's Rosita Gonzales," DJ said, nodding toward the woman. "She plays her guitar here and sings." Then he actually winked at the woman. "And she hears things. Tell 'em about the boat, Rosita."

The woman went on to explain in broken English how she'd overheard a conversation three nights earlier, about faking a boat theft.

"What do you mean they were going to *fake* a boat theft?" Charity asked her in Spanish.

The woman replied in whispered but rapid-fire sentences, then Charity turned toward the others.

"She said that one of the men was the owner of the boat," Charity told them. "He was with a man who is known locally—a man with snake and crocodile tattoos—who was supposed to be part of the South Pacific Cartel."

"Tell them where the boat is now," DJ prodded the woman.

"On *la playa*... How you say? The... sand? The beach! On the beach between Los Delfines and Mandalay."

"Those are two restaurants that share a common parking area just a little way up the beach from the pier," DJ added. "They both close way before midnight and the parking lot's empty. A good place to make a transfer from the boat to a waiting vehicle."

Exactly where I saw it go, Charity thought.

"Do you know the name of the man who owns the boat?" Kevin asked.

"*Si*," Rosita replied. "Is my no-good, cheating ex-husband, Manuel."

Oh, great, Charity thought, as she glanced at a dirty gray van that stopped outside. *Anything this woman tells us is tainted.*

The side cargo door to the van opened and Charity turned her head to look at it, assessing whether it was a threat or a delivery. The interior was dark, but she could just make out someone in the back. Then the door closed, and the van sped away.

"We should go check out this boat as soon as possible," Poppy suggested. "Before any clues that might be there are gone."

"If the police haven't already picked it up," Charity said. "If it *is* still there, it doesn't bode well for any police investigation."

"I must go back on stage," Rosita said to DJ. "Will you stay again?"

He smiled and leaned over to kiss her cheek. "I wish I could, honey," he replied. "You're a talented singer. But I gotta get back to work."

Charity's phone, sitting on the table by her elbow, pinged an incoming message. She opened it.

"It's Savannah," she said to Paul. "They just sent proof of life."

"What is it?" DJ asked, leaning closer.

"Still loading."

As soon as the image appeared, Charity dropped her phone on the table and sprinted toward the door, DJ right behind her.

"Gray cargo van," Charity said, looking eastward along the street.

DJ stepped past her, looking in the opposite direction.

"What is it?" Poppy asked, coming up beside Charity.

"We haven't been here two hours," Kevin said, extending Charity's phone to her. "And we've already been made."

"A dirty gray van stopped right here," Charity said. "Not three minutes ago. The sliding door on the side opened for a second and then it sped away."

Charity turned her phone so they could all see the screen. The image it displayed was from inside the van, where a frightened-looking Harper Landry sat facing the camera. In the background, through the open doorway of Coco Bongo, the six of them sat with Rosita Gonzales, Charity staring straight at the camera.

"There's no time stamp," Charity said. "The proof of life is that whoever took Harper knows that at least one of us is here."

142

CHAPTER SEVENTEEN

Charity's phone beeped in her hand. It was Savannah calling. She pressed the *Accept* button and put the phone to her ear.

"The boat they used was reported stolen," Charity told her without preamble, angry that they'd been spotted so easily. "But the woman here overheard her ex making a deal with Tattoo Man to use the ex's boat, then he'd report the theft this morning."

"I've had Chyrel monitoring phone calls from this part of Mexico to the United States," Savannah said. "Particularly to the New Orleans area, ever since you suggested the judge ask for proof of life."

Charity turned and walked a few steps to get away from the background noise.

"Savvy, the kidnapper sent that picture no more than four or five minutes ago," she whispered urgently, as she began to pace in front of the cantina. "Please tell me Chyrel got the number it was sent from."

DJ made a hand gesture and went back inside to pay for whatever he and Rosita had.

"The size of the file they sent allowed Chyrel time to get a good triangulation," Savannah said. "At the time it was sent , yes, the sender was just outside Coco Bongo. Did you see anyone?"

"No. The passenger window was tinted and the sliding cargo door on the side was open, but it was dark inside. I could only make out that there was someone sitting on the floor with their back to me. It had to be Harper. I was that close!"

"Chyrel is tracking the van now," Savannah said.

"Can you tell where it's going?"

"She's working on it, but there are only three cell towers in the area."

"Text me anything you find," Charity said.

"I'm wondering something..." Savannah said, letting the words trail off.

"What?"

"Judge Landry didn't even know who you were until just a little while ago," Savannah said thoughtfully. "Or that we were already working to get his daughter back."

Charity saw the connection instantly, or more precisely, the lack of a connection.

"You think the kidnappers weren't taking a proof-of-life picture with us in the background on purpose?"

"Maybe not you, DJ, or Paul," Savannah said.

"Good point," Charity said, looking over at Poppy and Kevin. Then her eyes went back to Rosita, the informant.

"Hang on," Savannah replied. "Chyrel's got something."

"Get in the car," Charity ordered everyone.

"Have DJ and Paul go check out the boat," Savannah said. "Chyrel is sending you the coordinates of where the phone is now. It's only approximate because it's outside the reception area of one of the three towers. But it was stationary for a few minutes before the signal was lost."

"Got it," Charity said, holding up a finger to DJ and Paul.

144

"What's the status on the satellite?"

"Still just a low angle view of the hilltops," Savannah replied. "Chyrel said she'll have eyes on the valleys in about an hour."

"Roger that," Charity said, and ended the call.

"Savvy wants you two to go check out the stolen boat," she told DJ. "She'll text us the location where the phone that sent the picture was last reported, and I'll go there and keep an eye on it. We might get lucky."

"Don't go charging in without us," DJ said.

"No plan to," she replied. "I'll just find a spot to conduct covert surveillance of the area—see if I can spot that van. Don't waste a lot of time on the boat. Odds are it's had people crawling all over it this morning."

"We'll go with you," Poppy said.

"Are you... armed?" Charity asked hesitantly.

"Well... no, but—"

"Get in," she said, climbing in the front passenger seat. "You two are extra eyes only."

Poppy nodded. "Understood." Kevin quickly opened the back door of the minivan for Poppy to get in.

Paul had already hailed a taxi from a stand a block down the road and the two men got in and it drove away, back the way they'd come.

"Where are we going now?" Enrique asked, smiling.

Charity's phone pinged an incoming message. It was from Chyrel, sending her an address and telling her the last known position of the phone that sent the picture was within two hundred feet of it.

Charity gave Enrique the address.

"That is a few kilometers outside Campeche," he advised. "In the Boxol Hills."

"Rough terrain?" Kevin asked, leaning forward in the back seat.

"Not so much," Enrique replied. "Low hills and dirt roads."

"Do you know if there's a high hill near that address?" Charity asked, pulling her camera case from the back to the floor in front of her.

He opened a navigation app on his phone and entered the address, then moved the map around with his finger.

"Yes," he replied, showing her the phone. "There is an old lean-to on top of this hill that overlooks the little valley where that address is located. It was once used to shoot coyotes from."

"Can you get to that hill in this minivan?" Charity asked. "I mean, without being seen by anyone at that address?"

"Yes," he replied, looking up with a grave expression. "I know those hills very well."

"Take us to the coyote shack," Charity said, grinning at Poppy and Kevin. She figured the mention of shooting coyotes for sport would get Poppy riled up, but if it did, she didn't show it.

Ten minutes later, Enrique stopped the van on a trail that was nothing more than two ruts through the surrounding scrub grass.

"The lean-to is just over there," he said, pointing ahead and to the right a little. "We must go on foot from here."

"You're not coming," Charity said. "If these people are cartel-connected, they will likely be armed. You're just a driver my boss hired. Nothing more. I don't want you getting hurt."

"I can take care of myself. I have a rifle."

Charity looked back at the other two and Kevin nodded.

"Get your rifle," Charity said, then got out and went around the passenger side with her camera case to meet him at the back of the vehicle.

Kevin and Poppy got out and joined them as Enrique lifted the cargo cover where the spare tire was kept. Nestled in the back, the butt of an antique-looking rifle stuck out of a blanket it was wrapped in.

"What is it?" Charity asked.

"I do not know who made it," he replied, uncovering the weapon. "But it fires the thirty caliber." He pulled it out and opened the bolt. "It is very accurate. That, I do know."

Kevin reached out and Enrique let him take the rifle. "You have a genuine World War II M-1 Carbine here, Enrique."

"You know how to use that?" Charity asked.

"Sure do," Kevin replied with a grin. "My dad has two just like this."

Charity pulled her Diamondback DB-9 from behind her back and extended it butt first to Poppy.

"You're going to cover us with the M-1?" she asked, palming the Diamondback.

"No," Charity said. "Enrique and his weapon are staying here with the car."

Charity watched as Poppy press checked the weapon, racking the slide back just enough to see the round in the chamber before gently releasing it. Then she dropped the magazine out and looked at the hollow point round on top.

"Only six rounds," Charity said to the younger agent. "But you can hide it anywhere. I use a thigh holster when I'm wearing a skirt."

"Then what will you use?"

Charity unzipped her camera case and lifted the telephoto lens out. She felt for the release under the foam padding, clicked it, put the lens back, and lifted the tray out.

"I have my own rifle," she replied, and in seconds she unfolded and assembled her rifle.

"Impressive," Poppy said. "Desert Tech bullpup?"

Charity nodded, appreciating the woman a bit more. "It's their SRS Covert model."

"I don't suppose you have one for me?" Kevin asked, handing Enrique back his rifle.

Charity mounted the long lens on one of the digital SLR camera bodies and handed it to him. "No. You're the eyes in the back of my head. Just make sure you duck if I swing around."

She quickly checked her phone again. No update from Chyrel. She made the gesture to follow, saw both Kevin and Poppy nod, then made her way to the lookout in a crouched run.

Once she found the best sight line, she lay down fully prone in the grass and propped herself on her elbows, slowly scanning the valley through the rifle scope. It wasn't her favorite shooting position, but Charity didn't anticipate firing a shot.

Poppy and Kevin found their own viewpoints within sight of Charity, and they waited.

And waited.

An hour later, they still hadn't seen anything move in the valley below.

Charity crawled on her elbows toward Poppy, and Kevin quickly joined them. "I assume you both have cell phones," Charity said. They nodded. "Since we don't have coms, give me your numbers. I'm going to head down there, do a walk around."

Poppy flipped the Diamondback around and handed it to Charity, then held out her hand for the rifle.

Charity hesitated, her gaze shifting to Kevin.

"It's okay. I get that all the time," Poppy said. "But you should know, I was the top shooter in my class at FLETC. The

148

marksmanship instructor said I was one of the top three he'd ever trained."

"The one out west?" Charity asked, handing over the rifle.

"Georgia," Poppy replied.

"No kidding?" Charity said, making no attempt to hide her surprise. "How did you cope with the smell from the paper plant?"

"Flavored lip balm," Poppy replied with a grin.

"Any field experience?"

Her gaze steady, Poppy said, "I've never killed anyone, if that's what you're asking."

"Well, let's hope you won't have to today."

She called Poppy's phone and once she'd answered, said, "Give me a slow ten-count."

Then she put her phone in her shirt pocket, buttoned it, and adjusted the volume through the material so she could barely hear Poppy counting.

"Kevin, find another viewpoint and call Poppy, so we'll all be on the line."

With her DB9 in a low ready position, Charity moved quickly down the hill, using what cover she could, and sprinting where she had none. Crouching behind a rock, she listened carefully.

"Do you see anything?" she whispered.

"Nothing," Poppy's muffled voice replied over the phone, barely audible.

Raising her head just enough to look over the rock, Charity noted the areas of cover between her and the small casita, the only structure in the valley.

Again, she moved down the rock-and-brush-strewn hillside, quickly learning that most of the stubby, thick underbrush had thorns.

The small house had no windows in back, which was odd, until she realized it faced a fairly steep hillside to the south and would get sun most of the year.

Charity angled toward the windowless side first.

The wall felt solid against her back, but the boards were bare, sun-bleached, and weathered by decades, if not centuries.

With her back to the wall, Charity moved slowly to her right, where she checked the windows on that side, and, seeing nothing, moved on to the front of the house. There was a porch that extended to both ends of the small dwelling, but she went back around and checked the windows on the east side before stepping up onto the porch.

Seeing nothing inside from the porch, she moved to the door. There was fine sand, almost like dust, on every surface, and the light breeze swirled and melted her tracks on the deck.

That same fine coating was on the doorknob.

"Clear," she said, moving toward the steps. "Nobody's been in this house in a while."

She went down the steps and out into the front yard, what there was of one. There was no fence anywhere in sight, just the shack and a double-rutted and overgrown trail that saw little use.

"There's nothing here," she said aloud, looking back at the front of the house. "And it doesn't look like anyone's been anywhere near here in..." A flash of light caught her eye out by the road. "Wait one."

She moved cautiously out to the side of the road, where it widened into three ruts, creating what would be a parking spot if it were anywhere else.

The lone piece of man-made material lay beside the wide spot and stuck out like a sore thumb.

Charity looked all around cautiously, then trotted toward it.

There were fresh tire tracks; apparently two cars had passed one another on the narrow double rut. Or they'd stopped side-by-side to talk. At the edge of the wide spot, she located the source of the reflected sunlight.

"Found a cell phone," she said, picking up a twisted and broken flip phone. "Or what's left of one."

"Does it work?" Poppy asked.

Charity held the phone up in the direction of the hilltop cover, holding it by one part, wires barely connecting it to the other. "I'm thinking probably not."

Her own phone trilled an incoming call and she took it out. "Savannah's calling," she said. "I'll patch her in."

She touched the screen and held the phone to her ear. "I'm at the location where the phone was last tracked," she said. "Agent McVie and Kevin are also on this line. There's nothing here except a busted cell phone."

"Do you remember the... uh, *associate* device Deuce uses to identify friends of a... person of interest?" Savannah asked vaguely.

She was referring to an electronic device an FBI agent who'd once worked with Deuce Livingston's DHS team had invented. Given a phone number, the device locked onto other cell phone signals that were active and in close physical proximity to the one being watched. If a number reappeared later or stayed close, it could be assumed it belonged to an associate of the suspect.

"Chyrel has another hit?"

"She does," Savannah replied. "She's texting the coordinates to you and DJ. He and Paul were about to leave the beach a moment ago, but the police arrived."

"That's not good," Charity muttered.

She knew Paul would play it cool, but DJ Martin was a loose cannon when it came to authority.

"They didn't find anything of use on the boat," Savannah said. "But they are being questioned, so it may be a while before they can join you."

"Where is this second location?" Charity asked, walking back toward the hill.

"It isn't far," Savannah replied. "Just a few miles inland from your present location."

"Send the numbers," Charity said. "We'll head that way and wait for backup."

CHAPTER EIGHTEEN

When Charity emerged from the woods with Poppy and Kevin, she found Enrique waiting at the back of the minivan. He was alert and looking down the road they'd driven up earlier.

Behind him lay his rifle, resting inconspicuously in the cargo area as he sat in the shade of the hatchback. Though it wasn't visible to anyone more than twenty feet down the hill, Charity felt sure the young man could have it up and ready before anyone got that close. There was nothing but barren landscape for a hundred yards in any direction.

"How long will it take us to get to Hacienda El Milagro?" Charity asked him as they approached.

He pointed in the direction of the little house in the valley where she'd found the mangled phone. "It is only a couple of kilometers from here." Then he pointed in the opposite direction. "But we have to go around the valley. About fifteen minutes."

Charity considered hiking it, knowing she could cover the distance much quicker—a little over a mile—but just as quickly, she discounted the idea, not wanting to be too far away from their transportation.

"Get in," she told the others, taking her rifle from Poppy and laying it in the back of the van with Enrique's.

"We are going to the ecological park?" Enrique asked.

"I think that's where they're hiding Harper," Charity replied.

He gave her an odd look. "It is a public place."

"How public?" Kevin asked.

Enrique shrugged. "I am sure it is open now. A few tourist groups go there each day. But it is never crowded."

Charity showed her phone to Enrique with the location Chyrel had sent her pinpointed on a terrain map. "Are there any other structures near there? A place where someone could hide out?"

He nodded somberly. "Your pinpoint is down the slope from the main buildings, and not a part of the park. There are some buildings there under the trees."

"Is there a fence separating it from the park?" Poppy asked.

"No," Enrique replied. "Young people used to go there to hang out."

They got into the van and, after backing up a hundred feet or so, Enrique found a spot where he could turn around.

"Nobody goes there to hang out anymore?" Poppy asked, looking out the side window. "An ecological park seems an odd place for a party spot."

"The park is somewhat new," Enrique replied, turning back onto the paved road and heading north.

"Is that when kids stopped hanging out there? Were they ousted by park rangers?"

He looked in the mirror at Poppy for a second before replying. "No. Two teenagers were murdered there a year ago, and now nobody goes back."

Charity glanced back at Poppy, wondering if she was suspecting the same thing—an early show of force by a cartel expanding into the area. She knew very little about what Poppy had encountered in her job, but Charity had been in deep with a couple of cartels and knew how ruthless they could be.

Murdering two innocent teens would send a message.

As Enrique steered the minivan at a snail's pace around curve after curve, Charity turned and looked out her window at the landscape going by.

This location seemed to fit. If the cartel had claimed that side of the park as their territory, no one would dare wander there. It would be secluded and fairly secure. It was an ideal location to keep a captive.

She looked down at the map on her phone, studying the terrain around the little red inverted teardrop. She had to find this girl and find her fast.

These types of kidnappings rarely ended well and everyone on their ad hoc team knew the odds, especially Savannah.

When Flo had been kidnapped, Charity had had a hard time helping Savannah hold it together, and her friend's desperation had become infectious. Now, Savannah was friends with the girl's mother, and she knew firsthand how badly she was suffering.

Charity wondered if she could maintain the objectivity she'd need.

To throw their personal issues into the mix was an added burden—it would just have to wait. She felt her gut clench.

Why had she done it? she wondered over and over. Jesse and Savannah were the best friends she'd ever had.

What is wrong with you? she asked herself.

After all this was done, she had to find a way to make amends, to tell Savannah how wrong she'd been, make her understand how sorry she was. She had to figure out a way. She had to.

"How do you want to do this?" Kevin asked, interrupting Charity's thoughts.

"Do what?"

"We can't very well just walk in brandishing rifles," he said.

Poppy nodded emphatically. "I doubt they'll be holding her in the main building. More likely in one of the others Enrique mentioned. And besides, whoever has Harper knows who we are. We can't just walk in anyway, guns or no guns. They'd scramble."

"Do you have a suggestion?" Charity asked, cursing herself for doing so.

"We pull a Doc Ford," Kevin replied. "We are who we are and we're in a place we'd be expected to be."

"And that's called a Doc Ford?" Poppy asked, beating Charity to the question.

"From the novels," he replied, as if that explained things. "You know. He's a mild-mannered marine biologist by day, who really works for the CIA or something, investigating stuff near the water. Nobody ever suspects him because of who he is and he's where he's supposed to be."

"And you two being wildlife cops," Charity said, "means you'd probably visit this place at some point?"

He shrugged. "We're not sure they know we're cops. Poppy and I have both been undercover for years as wildlife traffickers. If they've IDed us as our aliases, maybe they're wondering why we're here. If we walk in there, we could cast doubt, throw them a curveball. Especially since we can talk the talk."

"Or inflame the situation," Poppy said, turning to Charity. "Nothing personal, Charity, but a Girl Scout would make you in a heartbeat in a place like this."

"Makes better sense than what I had in mind, anyway," Charity said, glancing down at her phone again.

"What was your idea?" Kevin asked.

"Just... walk right in brandishing rifles," Charity replied. "And shoot the first person who also has a gun."

Enrique looked over at Charity and nodded. "The young couple that was murdered there," he said. "The girl was my cousin. The boy, the brother of my best friend."

Charity had had a feeling about Enrique since first meeting him. Just then she saw the pain in his eyes and could read his resolve. His people didn't like living under the cartels' bootheels, but there was little they could do about it. Dozens of Mexican drug cartels controlled vast amounts of cash, which the average police department couldn't resist. Wherever they operated, the cartels owned the law, from the chief to the meter maid. Those who didn't cooperate got sick and died, usually from lead poisoning. Those who did got relatively rich. The choice wasn't difficult.

"As much as I hate to admit it," Charity said, "the two of you *could* pull it off better than me. And if what you suspect is true about the cartel's running of illegal animals, and they *do* make your alias, who knows? You might make a deal and get inside to find Harper."

She waited for a straight part in the road, then showed Enrique her phone. "This looks like a bluff or cliff overlooking the park and the valley below."

"It is," he replied. "It is private property and was once a hunting preserve."

"Drop me off there," Charity said, then turned to the two wildlife agents. "All right. You two go in alone, do your thing, ask around, blend in, and see if you can find out anything. I want to get a bird's-eye view of the park and those buildings down below it. The park officials might not even know the cartel could be using it as a safe house."

Enrique turned onto another paved road, which ran fairly straight along a ridge, and five minutes later, he slowed and pulled to the shoulder.

"Go straight away from the road here," he said, pushing a button to open the rear hatch. "You will come to the bluff in four or five hundred meters."

Charity got out, then leaned back into the car and handed her pistol to Poppy. "Call my cell before you go in, so we can stay in contact."

"Will do," Poppy said. "Be careful."

Charity nodded, closed the door, then retrieved her rifle from the back of the van and closed the hatch.

As the van pulled back onto the road, she moved quickly into the woods, taking a bearing on the angle of the shadows cast by the sun, now halfway down to the western horizon.

When her phone vibrated in her pocket, she took it out, touched the *Accept* button, put it on speaker, then dropped it back into her pocket.

"We're in the parking lot," Poppy said.

"I'll be on the bluff to cover you in another couple of minutes," Charity replied.

She wasn't concerned about Poppy and Kevin's safety; they seemed to be able to handle themselves and it *was* a public place. But as she trotted through the sparse forest, she began to feel the unease creep into her consciousness.

What she was worried about was working *with* Poppy and Kevin like this. Or anyone, for that matter. Over the years, Charity had learned she worked best when she worked alone.

Poppy was still somewhat of a wild card in her mind. When they'd met that one time in Bimini, she'd seemed erratic and inexperienced.

Jesse had liked her; maybe he'd seen potential, or something Charity hadn't.

Or maybe he was just being an old horndog. Who knew? The thought alone gave her no sense of what she could expect from the young agent.

Kevin seemed capable, talked the talk, but she didn't know him either. And this "Doc Ford" idea made him seem a little edgy too. She'd have to keep a close eye on them both.

But should she alert Savannah to her concerns? Protocol dictated that she should. But what would she say?

Hey, Savvy, your husband had the hots for this Poppy, so I'm not sure we should trust his judgment.

That seemed pretty hypocritical, given the current situation, and considering her own issues.

Charity bent to a crouch and passed through a thick stand of brush, pushing the thorny branches away as best she could.

She knew that what *they* did was a lot different than what she did. She'd used an alias and had done some undercover work, sometimes deep, but *nothing* long term—she'd get in, do the job, and get out.

Maybe you had to be a little edgy with a crazy imagination to make it work long-term as a deep cover agent. After all, they went way in with no badge, no support, and no ID—only their wits—rubbing elbows with the worst of sleazy criminals. Their behavior could give them away in an instant. She also knew it would be doubly hard to pull off being young and attractive.

It probably took a certain kind of character to make it work, and Poppy had been deep undercover for years.

Hopefully, the personality traits it took to do that didn't include being a hothead as well.

It would take all of Charity's concentration to back them up if she didn't know what to expect.

CHAPTER NINETEEN

Emerging from a thicket of prickly shrubs that left red streaks on her forearms, Charity found herself on a low limestone bluff, several hundred feet higher than the wide valley floor extending ahead of her.

Scanning the valley quickly, Charity could easily make out the park buildings on another ridge, about four hundred yards away. That ridge was less steep and not nearly as high as the bluff she was on.

Looking northward, down that slope, Charity easily found the shack Enrique had mentioned, roughly a hundred feet below the park buildings and half a mile down slope.

The far side of the shallow valley was over a thousand yards away. Within range for the bullpup, but not by much. The park and the buildings were in the middle of the valley, though.

Beyond the next ridge, she could see other hilltops, but for the most part the terrain was relatively flat, with winding, shallow valleys called *arroyos* that could be anywhere from just deep enough to hide a person walking in a crouch to deep enough to hide a schooner.

Overall, the terrain wasn't all that dissimilar from Southern California, where Charity grew up. At least, once you got away from all the glitz of LA and moved inland.

She found a sandy spot next to a deadfall that would remain shaded the rest of the afternoon and began setting up her hide. In this case, it was little more than the opening between two parts of the tree trunk, which had likely already been dead when it fell, breaking in the middle on impact. The opening provided a parapet wall with a low area in the center.

The thought Savannah had had earlier about what the point of the proof-of- life photo was came back to Charity's mind as she worked at removing dead branches and rocks from where she planned to lie.

Armstrong Research took great pains in maintaining and updating their secure communications, and any call to or from one of Armstrong's cellular or satellite phones was encrypted and routed through Armstrong's own proprietary, multi-encrypted technical interface system, or METIS computer.

And she and Savannah were using Armstrong phones.

So there was no way the cartel had heard their conversation asking the judge to get proof that his daughter was still alive. And that proof had arrived within fifteen minutes of Judge Landry calling Jojo.

It was almost like they'd been driving Harper around in that gray van, maybe for hours, tailing them, waiting to get a picture.

But which one of us was the photographer's target?

If the cartel hadn't intercepted one of their calls, then someone in the group was known to them.

Poppy and Kevin had likely arrived in Campeche early that morning. And had probably flown under their real names. So their aliases wouldn't have popped up.

It was highly likely that it could be her. Charity had certainly made enemies south of the border. South of several borders. More

162

likely, they knew about Rosita. Charity frowned. It had to be her. If they suspected Rosita was an informant, she could be in danger.

Charity pushed more of the brittle wood away, widening and deepening the opening, then got prone behind it, with her rifle and left arm in the gap she'd created.

Getting comfortable on her belly, Charity spread her legs and then brought her right leg up high in what was called the leg-up prone position. By keeping the leg on the weapon side cocked, it was easier to roll that side of the body up for better stability behind the scope. It had the added benefit of making it faster to get to your feet.

She removed the lens covers and was just bringing the scope to the main buildings when Poppy's voice came over the phone in her pocket.

"We struck out here," she said. "The park's about to close and the people we talked to seem oblivious to anything going on."

"You went in already?" Charity asked, a bit irritated that they hadn't waited for her to get into position.

She could see the two of them outside the entrance, thirty feet or so from Enrique's van. But they weren't walking toward it. Instead, Kevin was pointing toward a road a hundred feet to the left of the building that ran down the hill toward the shack.

"I have an idea," Poppy said, ignoring Charity's question.

When she explained her idea, Charity didn't like it at all. She'd be able to provide ample coverage, but with just the three of them, they'd be spread pretty thin. Even if Enrique volunteered himself and his rifle, they'd have three guns between the four of them.

Cartels were virtual civilian criminal armies. They would have automatic weapons, even machine guns mounted in the beds of pickups. These were called technicals, and a good driver with a good off-road vehicle could make the machine gunner in the back a very deadly and formidable foe.

"Let me get Savvy on the line," Charity said. "See how far out DJ and Paul are."

"Fair enough," Poppy said. "We don't mind being part of the team, but could you clear up a little confusion here? Who's in charge of this op? You or Savannah?"

"Savannah."

"Well, if you don't mind me saying, and it's just me reading body language, but there's some tension between you two," Poppy said. "None of my business, but if things heat up, we want to know there's not a problem between you and your boss."

"She's not my boss," Charity said. "She's a friend, and we just happened to both be near here when the kidnapping took place. She's been assigned lead."

"But you're friends and–"

"She's Jesse McDermitt's wife," Charity said, as she tapped Savannah's name on her call list, hoping that revelation would end the discussion.

"Jesse's wife?" Poppy said.

"What's going on?" Savannah asked, sounding all business. "Chyrel is telling me you separated from Kevin and Poppy."

"They're on the line with us," Charity replied. "With no comms, we're just using open calls on our cells. Where are DJ and Paul?"

"Still at the beach with the police," Savannah replied. "Have you found anything there?"

"Kevin and I went in and asked around," Poppy replied, a bit stiffly. "If the cartel is using the shack down in the valley, I don't think anyone with the park knows about it."

"Chyrel has the satellite close enough now that I have a good view of your location," Savannah said. "I can see Poppy and Kevin clearly."

"I'm on a low, heavily wooded bluff a little over a quarter mile to their north-northeast," Charity said. "I have the whole valley covered. We just need DJ and Paul here. We have one rifle and a handgun between the three of us. Are you still able to track the location of the associate phone?"

"It's still pinging in the same spot," Savannah replied. "Zooming in on it, I see two buildings, one large and one small."

"I only see one," Charity said, sweeping the scope back to the shack.

"The larger building is to the northeast of the smaller one," Savannah advised. "It might be blocking your view."

Charity lifted her head and looked along the edge of the bluff she was on for a better position. It was crowded with the thorn bushes, and she didn't see any openings to move through. She looked back through the scope, studying the building she could see.

"I really can't move laterally for a view of both," Charity said.

"The satellite's almost directly opposite," Savannah said. "Between us, we can see everything."

Without warning, a large door opened on the shed, and a man came out.

"I have movement on the east side of the larger building," Charity announced, watching the man through her scope.

Charity realized the building was more of a barn than any kind of living quarters. She saw the back of what looked like a gray van before the man closed the door and walked around the building, disappearing.

"Someone is crossing between the two buildings," Savannah said. "The only thing I can say for sure is that the person is dark-skinned and walks like a man."

"It is a man," Charity said. "I saw him close enough to see facial hair. And I think the gray van is in the bigger building. I caught a glimpse inside before he closed the door."

"He disappeared into the smaller building," Savannah advised.

Charity studied the building she could see. If it was a barn, it wasn't built in the traditional way with an arched roof, but had just a single flat, metal roof, sloped slightly toward the back.

A garage of some kind, she thought. *Or a tractor shed?*

This wasn't exactly farm country, though. Utility buildings for whatever was there before the park?

"I still think my plan will work," Poppy said. "And I'm sure I can BS my way out, if I have to."

"What plan is that?" Savannah asked.

"Well, there are several hiking trails around the park," Poppy began. "I think we can wander into the camp, and if we're seen, we'll make like we're lost hikers. It's a good, plausible story."

"Maybe," Savannah asked, a tinge of doubt in her voice. "But can you sell it?"

Through her scope, Charity saw Poppy shrug and reply, "It's what I do."

Kevin chimed in. "I can vouch for her. She had me snowed."

"Do you think it might be just as plausible if you went in alone?" Savannah asked. "A lone woman would be less threatening."

Charity could see Poppy looking at Kevin. He shook his head.

"Alone?" Poppy asked.

"Yes. I'd rather have Kevin nearby as back-up with the pistol. Charity will have you covered from the ridge. And most importantly, you'll be much less of a threat and more believable. Do you agree?"

Kevin shook his head again.

"Agreed," Poppy said.

166

"I'm opposed," Charity said. "We should wait for DJ and P—"

"Neither of them is armed," Savannah replied, a bit curtly. "That's our gray van you saw. Time is of the essence and somebody in that building was with the kidnapper when he sent the proof-of-life photo. Harper could very well be in there right now."

What Savannah said made tactical sense.

The terrain Charity saw through her scope was rough and mostly treeless, and as strong as DJ was, a one-legged man and a psychologist, both unarmed, wouldn't be much benefit.

But it would be risky as hell for just the three of them.

She'd much rather wait until dark and have Deuce and some of his SEAL buddies make a HALO insertion with night vision and automatic weapons, while she and Kevin rushed the other side of the camp with rifles.

But that wasn't possible right now.

While Charity watched from the bluff and described what she could see, Kevin, Savannah and Poppy came up with a plan that utilized the terrain to their advantage.

Kevin went over to Enrique's van to tell him what they were doing, and make sure he stayed put until they returned.

Then Poppy went west around the park's main buildings, to a small *arroyo*, then disappeared down into it.

Charity scanned the area downhill and spotted a flash of red hair as Poppy made her way toward the camp. A few minutes later, she spotted her once more, her hair again giving her away against a backdrop that was mostly brown and gray. She was slightly past the camp, where the *arroyo* started to flatten out into the valley basin.

"Okay, I'm in position," Poppy said, her voice over the cell phone only slightly muffled inside Charity's pocket.

"I can see you clearly," Charity said. "As well as the ground between you and the shacks."

"Poppy, stay cool. You've got this," Kevin told her. "Give me another few minutes to move into a better position. I'm due east of you in a bunch of rocks."

The seconds ticked past as Charity scanned the area east of Poppy's position, looking for Kevin. It took a minute to find him, and she only saw him for a second.

"The satellite is giving me a clear view now," Savannah said. "I can see Kevin across the clearing from you, Poppy, no more than fifty or sixty feet from the shack."

"I'll need radio silence, but it'd be good if you guys listened in. I'll just turn down my volume, so nobody else can hear you."

Through her rifle scope, Charity watched Poppy make the adjustment on her phone, and then Savannah said, "Can you hear me now?"

Poppy didn't react, then stepped out of cover and started walking slightly away from Charity's position, angling away from the shack.

"She didn't react," Charity said. "And she's moving in."

As Poppy approached the larger structure, she slowed, her shoulders slumped forward, as if exhausted from the late afternoon heat.

"Thank God!" Charity heard her say, rather loudly. "Shelter from the sun. Please let there be water inside."

She added a convincing stumble.

Charity grinned. Walking into a possible cartel lair with no weapon and very little backup took a lot of guts.

Especially knowing that it made *her* a target for kidnapping, also.

Maybe she'd underestimated Poppy. Or maybe she was

absolutely nuts and would get them all killed.

Charity kept the scope centered on the ground between Poppy and the shack. She was circling wide to her left, approaching it more from the north and east, to draw anyone out of the smaller building and into Charity and Kevin's line of fire.

"Damn!" Savannah hissed on the phone.

Charity watched closely to be sure Poppy hadn't reacted to the break in silence. "What's wrong?"

"Someone spotted her," Savannah said. "He's moving toward her from behind, fifty feet northeast."

Charity moved the scope downward and spotted a man with his back to her, staying low and moving from rock to rock toward the unsuspecting wildlife agent. She couldn't see if he was armed or not.

"He's got a gun!" Savannah said in alarm. "He's going to shoot her."

"Weapon confirmed," Kevin whispered. "Way too far for me, and Poppy's between us."

"Stay calm," Charity whispered, adjusting her aim to compensate for the low trajectory and light wind. "If he was going to shoot unseen, he would've done it already. Watch his body language, Savvy. He's probably just going to confront her. We anticipated this might happen."

Charity continued to hold the reticle centered on the man's right hip, knowing the wind would push her round to center and the negative declination would put it in the middle of his back.

"He's moving closer!" Savannah said. "He was within challenging distance when I first saw him!"

"His body language doesn't appear threatening yet," Charity said in a calm voice. "I have him covered, but can't see his face or weapon."

"It's a pistol," Savannah said. "He's getting closer!"

Charity could hear the nerves in her friend's voice. This case was too personal, too close to home.

This was a bad idea, Charity thought.

Why Stockwell had put Savannah in charge, she didn't know. He must have had his reasons. But right now, it was clear to Charity that Savannah couldn't be objective. She was as jittery as a cat on a wire.

Charity gently pressed the trigger, removing the slack, anticipating having to take control herself.

"He's raising his gun!" Savannah shouted. "Take the shot! Take the shot!"

Shit.

Time slowed. Charity felt the release of the trigger and heard the hammer strike the firing pin. The Lapua .308 match-grade cartridge in the chamber fired. She felt the recoil as a flash of expanding powder erupted from the muzzle. The rifle made a deafening bark, ejecting the spent cartridge and loading another.

Charity knew the sound would be heard all through the valley, but she felt sure that the direction wouldn't be immediately discernible.

Until she took a second shot. Hopefully it wouldn't be needed.

With the action behind the trigger, the bullpup didn't have a lot of barrel rise, and the scope came back down just as her round reached its target.

The man lurched forward, as if he were being snatched up by his shirt front.

A fine pink mist emanated from his chest, painting the nearby rocks in frothy red foam.

He was dead before his body thudded, face-first, to the ground, dust swirling around his left shoulder.

CHAPTER TWENTY

Waves of nausea kept coming. The heat, the constant movement, the blindfold. Harper felt as if she were in Hell. A never-ending misery. Hope had left her.

It seemed all they did was drive around. Then move to another vehicle, then drive around some more, sometimes stopping for an hour or two at an abandoned building or shack. Then change to a different vehicle and a different driver. She was sure they had different drivers because they would say a few words, and even blindfolded, Harper could tell. They didn't talk much, usually just something like, "how long?" or "which direction?" She was sure their voices were different.

Except for the tattooed man. He was always with her.

The first time they'd removed her blindfold, he had shown her his gun, told her he was always watching, that she'd better behave. "If you are a good girl, you can go home to your daddy," he'd told her at one place they'd stopped.

Something about the way he said it didn't make her feel any better. She hadn't done anything to deserve this, and she was sure there was nothing she could do to change their minds about it.

All she could do was hope and pray. And, sometimes, when she could slow her breathing and tamp down the terror, think.

She had little to go on, but Harper had taken Spanish classes all through high school and college. She didn't want to let them know she understood anything. Somehow, that made her feel like she had some advantage, as futile as it probably was.

But they rarely spoke. When they'd taken her picture, the driver had said something about a horse—a red horse. The building had been red. Maybe it was called the Red Horse Cantina or something.

But what did that have to do with her?

Why her?

She retraced her steps since she'd been in Mexico. They'd only gone to shore a few times, to shop and get coffee, then lounge on the beach.

If you are a good girl, you can go home to your daddy.

This had to be about her dad. Otherwise, why mention her dad at all? When she was taken, she'd been with her mom. Her dad hadn't come to Mexico with them. How did they even know she had a dad?

Was the mention of her father a cultural thing? She remembered how her Spanish teacher had explained that the Mexican culture was patriarchal. Was that the reason?

But Tattoo Man knew her name. He could've overheard her mom call her by her name. But he would have had to be close and following them. But why? Random target? She'd been warned about that. But they'd been so careful.

Maybe this whole thing really *was* about her dad. All they had to do was Google his name and they'd know hers. But how would they have known she was in Mexico?

She supposed if Tattoo Man knew who she was, then he could figure out how to call her dad for money. That had to be it. They would call him for ransom. Wasn't that the point of kidnapping someone? That was the only thing that made sense.

She wasn't sure if that made her feel better or worse. If they demanded money, and her dad couldn't pay, then what?

One thing seemed certain; these men were professionals. They seemed to know exactly what they were doing. No arguing, like in the movies. No long discussions. They seemed to have some kind of network, the way she was constantly transferred from vehicle to vehicle, place to place. Was that normal? Or did they have to keep moving because someone was already looking for her?

Though they seemed to act like professionals, they didn't exactly have the best accommodations or most reliable transportation. It seemed almost as if they were winging it, using whatever they had at their disposal. That didn't fit with their attitude and communication.

Then again, what did she know about kidnapping? Only that it was terrifying, and she wished the nightmare would be over soon.

Finally, they stopped at a location where she had the feeling they were planning to stay for a while. She was given water to drink and a small bowl of cold beans. When they allowed her to take her blindfold off, the building she saw seemed to be like someone's house. There were dishes by a wash tub and chickens in the yard.

They allowed her to use a bathroom, if one could call it that. She thought of it more as an indoor outhouse with a straw cloth hanging for a door. But at least they let her go.

As she stood from the toilet, she noticed through a narrow gap between two planks that there was another house nearby where a man worked a square of soil with a hoe. Could she get to him? Would he help her?

She eased the cloth back. Tattoo man was looking the other way. A surge of adrenaline pulsed through her veins. This was her chance. She bolted for the door, ran through it and into the sunlight toward the man.

A gun shot blasted her ears. She tumbled to the ground, her face skidding across gravel. Then the terror came, in a flash of realization. He would kill her now.

What had she been thinking? Her jaw began to quiver and she couldn't breathe. She gulped for a breath. Someone kicked her in the side. She rolled over, squinting into the sun. Then a shadow passed across her eyes.

Tattoo Man stood over her.

A quick glance toward the other man told her all she needed to know. He kept hoeing, as though he hadn't heard a thing, his eyes glued to the ground.

Tattoo Man grabbed hold of her hair and yanked her to her feet. Searing pain burned her scalp. She grabbed at her head, trying to hold her hair to keep it from pulling out at the roots.

He pushed her back toward the house. He didn't say anything. He didn't have to.

Once inside, he shoved her into a chair and lashed her wrists behind her back.

"*Puta!*" he spat.

She knew that word. Not that it mattered. For a while, she had clung to any words they'd spoken. But it wasn't like there was anything she could do with that information. At some point, they were sure to kill her.

CHAPTER TWENTY-ONE

Charity was already sliding down the side of the rocky bluff when Savannah screamed and yelled for her and Kevin to move in. It wasn't steep but the rocks made for slow going.

When she reached the bottom, she broke into a sprint, leaping over rocks and dodging shrubs. Kevin came out of the rocks just ahead of her, also running to where Poppy was kneeling beside the dead man. When Kevin got to her, he stood with his back to her, looking for further threats.

Charity reached them and she and Kevin stood back-to-back, with Poppy and the body between them, weapons up, ready to shoot anything that moved.

Charity's adrenaline had spiked when she felt the recoil from the shot, and she knew that was what was making her hyperaware, her mind noting and recording every detail, as if in slow motion.

"*No dispares! Por favor, no me mates!*"

Charity and Kevin both turned toward the threat.

"Come out now!" Kevin yelled back, pointing Charity's pistol in the direction the voice had come from.

"*Sal, ahora! Manos en la cabeza!*" Charity added, to make sure he understood.

Poppy rose into a crouch, unarmed but ready.

A man came slowly from the smaller building, his hands on his head as Charity had ordered him. He was older, with graying hair and deep lines carved into a weathered face.

"*No soy cartel*," he said, stopping twenty feet away.

"That guy cartel?" Kevin asked, nodding his head sideways toward the body of the man who'd almost shot Poppy.

"*Sí, señor*," he replied, then turned toward Charity with pleading eyes. "I am... *pescador*," he attempted in English, searching for the word fisherman.

Charity slowly lowered her rifle, but Kevin kept the man covered. She turned her head slowly, examining the small house and the area around it.

"Is he... dead?" Savannah croaked, her voice emanating from both her and Kevin's phones.

Charity looked down at the body, which Poppy had rolled over. There was a big hole where his heart used to be, if he'd ever had one.

"Very dead," Poppy replied, then looked up at Charity. "Thank you."

Charity could hear strange sounds from her pocket.

Was Savannah sobbing?

"Are you okay?" she asked, meaning both Poppy and Savannah.

"Yeah," Poppy replied, then pointed to the man from the shack. "What do we do with the fisherman?"

"Savannah, are you all right?" Charity asked.

There was only silence.

Charity turned and walked straight toward the second man, her muzzle intentionally pointed at his chest. The barrel rose as she got closer, until it was under the man's chin.

"Is the girl here?" she asked him in Spanish, her voice calm, but with a menacing tone.

"*No, señora,*" he replied, his voice cracking in fear as his whole body trembled. *Por favor, señora.*

He spoke some English, but it was faster if Charity translated what he said for the others. "The other cartel man took her away in a car. He says he only drives the van."

"The gray van?" Kevin asked him.

His eyes conveyed confusion. "*No, señor.* Is not gray. *Es azul...* er... blue."

It was blue?

Charity moved toward the larger building where she'd seen the van to get a look for herself. But when she swung the door open, the barn was empty.

Why had she thought she'd seen a van? There was nothing but remnants of straw in the corner. A couple of shelves held several cans, some turned on their sides, all covered with spider webs.

As near as she could tell, the two buildings had once been a small farmhouse and barn, though what the original occupants might have grown was a mystery.

She turned back toward the others. "Everyone inside," she ordered, motioning toward the smaller building. "Kevin, drag that body into the bushes and hide it, then join us."

Kevin nodded, lifted the dead man's legs, and began dragging the body across the gravel.

Poppy bent and picked up the dead man's revolver and pointed it at the fisherman. "Move," she ordered. "*Dentro de la casa.*"

The three walked to the smaller structure, which Charity could now see was indeed someone's abandoned living quarters, with a porch running the width of the front of the house. She doubted it was the fisherman's, which she confirmed when she pulled the door open on squeaky hinges.

Inside, she found a one-room domicile with no furniture or any sign of running water or a toilet. Completely abandoned, but signs of obvious squatters.

It was built with brick at the base and weathered plank exterior walls above the brick, exposed on the inside, as was the rusted, corrugated metal roof. It might have once had two interior walls, judging by a line of exposed nails in the rafters. Three windows had been boarded closed from the inside—the wall without a window faced south.

If anyone had been held there, the heat must have been unbearable.

Charity stepped back outside and took her phone from her pocket. She disconnected Poppy and Kevin from the call.

"Can you see any sign of hostiles, Savvy?"

"We're not seeing any."

It was Chyrel.

"Where's Savvy?" Charity asked, alarmed.

"She um... had to step away. I hacked into your phone call until she gets back and I'm watching the satellite feed. Looks like the park's closed up. Just your driver in his van. Nothing else moving anywhere near you."

"She had to step away?" Charity asked. "Right now?"

"Yeah," Chyrel replied. "She seemed really shook up on my live video feed, Charity. I'm not real sure... I don't know... Is she even up for this?"

Without a handler, Charity immediately took control. Her mind clicked into gear, setting aside her personal concern for Savannah.

"I want a half-mile perimeter watch," Charity directed. "Including IR and motion sensor. Can you jam all cell phones in this area?"

"Roger that," Chyrel responded. "VHF and UHF, too. And FYI, Paul and DJ are five minutes out."

"Thanks. Keep this line open, as well as theirs and Poppy's and Kevin's."

"Will do."

Charity returned her phone to her shirt pocket and stepped back inside the shack.

Poppy had the fisherman on his knees with his hands bound behind his back.

"Are you all right?" she asked Poppy again.

The woman *had* just had a man cut down several feet behind her. Charity had known seasoned veterans who'd been shaken by less.

"Yeah. I've checked. No weapon on this guy. But he's got a phone."

Charity nodded. *Okay, she's all business.*

Poppy handed the phone to Charity. It was a cheap flip phone, much like the one she'd found destroyed at the last place they looked. Probably the phone they'd tracked here, since Poppy didn't report finding one on the body.

"It is not mine," the fisherman said in Spanish. "I was given it and mine was taken. They call me and tell me where to go."

Poppy rose and patted the fisherman on both shoulders. "He's clean."

Charity glanced around at the disheveled, dirt-floor interior, strewn with trash and a couple of torn and stained sleeping bags.

She grinned at Poppy. "That's debatable."

Kevin stepped through the door and went straight to Poppy. "Are you okay?" He pointed his weapon at the man. "I've got this. Why don't you sit down. Take a breather."

Yep, he's smitten, Charity thought. *Always complicates things.* She hoped it wouldn't become a problem here.

She turned her attention to the man. "Did you see the girl, Harper?"

He shook his head.

"When I asked before, you said she was gone, that another man took her in a car."

"*Si,*" he replied, "*supongo.*"

"He supposes," Poppy translated for Kevin.

"Yeah." Charity switched to Spanish. "*Dónde está tu vehiculo?*"

"*No aqui.*" He explained their system as best he could.

"They change cars and change drivers. No choice. I get it." Charity nodded and asked in Spanish, "The cartel is in control here?"

He also nodded, then lowered his head, as if in shame.

Chyrel's voice came from Charity's pocket. "Paul and DJ are approaching."

"Have their driver leave them," Charity said. "We need to camp out here and wait for this guy's ride to return. And it's probably safer if our driver, Enrique, comes down with them. He has an old rifle with him."

"Do you think anyone heard you shoot?" Chyrel asked. "Of course, we couldn't *hear* anything, watching from a satellite camera. But Savannah and I both saw it."

Charity remembered the angle the satellite had been watching from, almost due south. Savannah had been able to see the man from the front. She'd seen the result of her order to take the shot—the man's chest exploding when Charity's bullet ripped through his body.

"I'm sure a few people did," Charity replied. "But even though the valley isn't deep, I don't think anyone hearing it could've determined the direction."

"What if someone says something to the cartel?"

"I hope they do," Charity replied. "Then they'll call, not get through, and come to investigate."

CHAPTER TWENTY-TWO

Savannah heard the loud crack from her cell phone's speaker when Charity fired. She watched in horror as the man she'd spotted with the satellite's camera seemed to be yanked forward, blood bursting from his chest as he fell face down in the dirt.

She pushed back from the laptop and screamed.

In an instant, it was done.

Savannah sat motionless, her hand over her mouth. Time seemed to slow as she gazed at the image on the laptop.

She'd given the order.

The threat was down. Eliminated. Neutralized.

Had I made the correct call? she wondered, doubt flooding her mind. Maybe Charity had been right, and he *was* only coming out to talk. He had a weapon, but that didn't mean he was about to use it.

What if he was their only link to find Harper?

Oh God!

The man lay in the dirt, face down, stone still. Yet she couldn't get the violent image out of her mind—the man's chest had exploded. She hadn't expected that. She'd seen men die, but had never pulled the trigger or given the order.

Chyrel's voice came over her headset in a hushed whisper. "Now what?"

A terror rose in Savannah's chest. Now they were exposed. What if he wasn't the only one?

"Move in! Move in!"

Oh God! She could be sending them all into a trap! What if it's a bloodbath?

Thousands of thoughts crashed into one another in Savannah's mind as her heart raced out of control.

Suddenly, she thought of Jesse. He'd done this for over forty years! *How did he carry the pain? The guilt?*

On the screen in front of her, she watched as Charity sprinted down the hill and Kevin emerged from the rocks at a dead run. Kevin reached Poppy first, pistol raised, standing over her in a protective way.

Then Charity stopped next to Poppy also, facing the opposite way from Kevin.

They're professionals, she thought. They know what they're doing. They've done this before.

She could see her friend's face clearly on the screen, brow furrowed, head and eyes moving, missing nothing.

Head on a swivel, she heard Jesse's voice echo in her mind.

She took a man's life! How is she so composed, so self-confident? So... unfazed?

Poppy was on the ground. Why was she on the ground?

Savannah touched the mute icon on her phone, lying beside the laptop, and looked around.

She was alone in *MollySue's* cockpit for now. The sliding glass door was closed. Everyone was eating and nobody had heard her scream.

Did I scream? Of course she had; she screamed at spiders.

She pulled her headset mic closer, whispering urgently to

184

Chyrel. "Was she hit? Oh no! Was Poppy hit? Check the angle of Charity's shot."

"No, Savannah!" Chyrel insisted. "I'm sure she wasn't. Charity would have known not to—"

"Come out now!" Kevin's voice yelled from the cell phone's speaker, startling her.

On the screen, Savannah saw Poppy rise quickly into a crouch, unarmed but ready. She looked unhurt.

Charity and Kevin both turned toward the smaller shack, weapons trained on it.

"*Sal, ahora! Manos en la cabeza!*" Charity instructed.

A man stepped out from behind the building, hands on his head.

Savannah's hand went to her mouth. Another man? Of course there was more than one.

But now there wasn't.

She'd ordered the first man to be killed.

Savannah looked up at the pastel colors of the sky as the sun neared the horizon. *Oh dear Lord, what have I done?*

The image on the screen zoomed in on the man's back, Chyrel controlling the camera.

Savannah suddenly felt her stomach turn. Would she see this second man shot down, as well? Would his back explode from Charity's bullet?

"That guy cartel?" Kevin asked, nodding toward the body at Poppy's feet.

Charity slowly lowered her rifle and looked around, but Kevin kept the man covered.

Savannah shot up from her chair. "What's going on? Why did Charity lower her weapon? There could be more!"

Chyrel answered. "Charity has the rifle, Savannah. Kevin has the pistol, and has the man covered."

"Yes, but..."

"It's standard procedure."

Her gaze went back to the man lying prone in the dust behind the group. Had he moved? No, of course he hadn't. His chest had been blown out the front of his shirt. Her stomach tightened again as she clicked to turn off mute.

"Is he... dead?" she croaked.

"Very dead," Poppy replied, looking down at the body, then up at Charity. "Thank you."

Tears welled up in Savannah's eyes and burst forth without warning.

Oh God!

The room began to spin. The back of her throat tightened, and her stomach suddenly contracted.

She stumbled backward. The headset was yanked from her head by the cord, clattering to the floor. She spun and took one step as the bile rose in her throat.

"Savannah! Savannah!" Chyrel's tinny voice came from the headset's earphone.

Savannah could hear, but she couldn't process.

Finally, she picked the headset up and held the mic to her mouth. "I need a minute."

"But they're on the ground. They haven't secured the scene."

"I need a minute," she repeated, then dropped the headset as stomach acid rose in her throat again. She rushed to the side of the cockpit and vomited into the sea.

The vision of the man's insides blowing out the front of his shirt kept playing back in her mind as her stomach involuntarily emptied itself.

When she felt spent, she slumped to the deck, her back against the gunwale, eyes blurry and unfocused.

"I just... I just killed a man," she whispered and started sobbing again. "Dead. He's dead."

The tears came again, unbidden.

Jojo appeared suddenly from the salon and rushed toward her.

"Oh my God!" he cried out. "Are you all right? What has happened? Is it Harper?"

Savannah shoved herself upright against the gunwale. "No, no. It's not her. We just... I don't know about her. She... I need to get back to the comm."

Savannah shifted to get up.

"But something has happened," Jojo said softly, putting a hand on her shoulder. "Something is very wrong, obviously."

"Yes," she replied, her eyes brimming again. "It was necessary. I need to..."

Jojo took her by the arm and helped her to her feet. She grabbed her water bottle to get the taste out of her mouth.

"Please tell me what has happened. Was she there?"

"I don't know. I need to get back. I just..." She glanced around the deck at her feet. She needed to get her bearings. "I just had to have a moment. Just a moment. I'm okay."

His gaze was intense as his eyes searched hers.

"It just got hot," she said. "I had to make a decision. It was... necessary."

She couldn't hold back the tears.

Jojo reached his arm around her and drew her into his embrace. "This whole situation is a nightmare," he whispered softly. "You are doing your best. We all know that. Please tell me what has happened to put you in such a state."

She sniffled, trying to gain control of her feelings. "Thank you," she managed to say.

He pulled back to look into her eyes. "What can I do to help?"

"Nothing. I mean, this meant a lot. Thank you. But I need to get back. There is one thing I'd like you to do for me, though."

"Anything."

"Go check on Alberto for me?"

"He is downstairs," Jojo replied. "I was just with him a few moments ago."

"I know," she said, managing a smile. "I just need you to."

He smiled back at her. "I understand."

CHAPTER TWENTY-THREE

The house smelled of piss, stale tobacco smoke, and liquor, probably rotgut tequila. It was apparent that men had spent a lot of time there recently, doing a lot of nothing.

Just waiting. But waiting for what?

Now Charity was the one doing the waiting. And she hated waiting.

She believed the fisherman was just doing what he was told, probably at the threat of harm to his family.

Paul and DJ had finally arrived, along with Enrique, who was sitting on the porch just outside the open door.

Savannah had rejoined the call, and she and Chyrel were monitoring two different satellite feeds. Chyrel was watching through a heat filter, which would work amazingly well in the sparse landscape, as the rocks cooled once the sun went down. Savannah used only magnified ambient light, and with a full moon shining down into the valley, she'd said she could see quite well.

When she'd returned to the comm, she'd sounded shaken, but controlled. For the last hour she'd only briefly reported the occasional vehicle that drove past the park entrance.

DJ was pacing like a captive tiger, moving from the door to a crack between the slats on one of the windows, scanning outdoors.

Kevin and Poppy had volunteered to take the first watch for anyone coming down the two-track, while Charity checked the house for any clues. She'd found nothing.

Paul's calm voice seemed to emanate from between the wooden slats, though he was only ten feet away. "You seem tense."

"Yep, I'm tense," she said with a wink. "Good observation."

"It's just that I've never known you to be this worked up before."

"No?" she said, looking away. She didn't need this right now. "You get the after-action reports, do you?"

He smiled benignly. She knew that he was aware she worked alone, and he'd never been on any assignment with her since their DHS days with the Caribbean Counterterrorism Command.

"Are there any concerns you're not sharing?" he asked.

"Nope."

"Perhaps you're not comfortable working with the other agents. You hadn't *seemed* comfortable with agent McVie when she arrived."

His statement sounded like a question. But obviously it wasn't. Charity had dealt with her fair share of analysts and psychologists. He was psych-baiting her—a term of her own concoction for this sort of psycho-babble.

"Maybe," she said, trying to sound noncommittal. "I know I work better alone."

"Um-hm."

She stopped and turned to face Paul. "What does that mean?"

"He's just tryin' to help," DJ said, stopping his pacing for a moment. "He's helped me deal with some issues."

Paul returned Charity's gaze with soft eyes. "I'm agreeing with you. You prefer to work alone. Nothing wrong with that."

"That's right."

"And you usually work without direct supervision. No one to

190

answer to, I mean. Make your own decisions in real time."

"Usually," she replied, wondering what he was getting at. "Not always."

He would know all that if he'd opened even page one of her file, and she had the suspicion he'd gone deeper than that.

She had no time for this and strode toward him, stopping only when her face was inches from his. Then she studied him with fiery eyes.

"I'm a take-charge kind of woman," she said, looking him up and down. Maybe aggression would throw him off and stop his needling.

"Yes, that's very clear," Paul said, calmly stepping back to maintain his personal space.

Charity smiled.

"No need to go gettin' hostile," DJ interrupted.

"What I don't like is a lack of communication," Charity said, still addressing Paul. "So, tell me. What's your story?" She moved closer to him again, an offensive posture she hoped would make him back down. "Why are you here? The judge has made it very clear he wants Jojo handling any negotiation."

A small smile crossed Paul's lips. "You know as well as I do, when Jack Armstrong summons, you come."

"That doesn't explain why you're here."

"I know," he said, holding her gaze.

"Well, nothing personal," she mumbled, trying to get some footing. "But you're a liability."

"Oh. Am I?"

"Too many people involved, too many mistakes that can be made. There are six of us and only three guns. I know you used to be on the presidential detail, but that's literally all you could do here;

step in front of a bullet." After a beat, she added. "And you're distracting me from my work."

"I'm sorry. I thought we were simply waiting. And we could chat."

"You know me well enough to know I'm not interested in chitchat."

DJ stopped pacing and turned to Paul. "Chatty Cathy she ain't."

"Indeed. That's quite obvious."

"Then why do you persist?" Charity asked him.

"Stubbornness, I guess."

"She's got ya beat in the stubborn department too, Doc," DJ said.

"Ah, yes. DJ, I had the impression you two know each other quite well. I mean, much better than— well— than I would have thought."

Charity held back an eye roll.

"Whatcha gettin' at, Doc?" DJ said, his face screwed up into a grimace as he stepped toward Paul.

Charity put a hand on DJ's chest, not taking her eyes from Paul's. "He's saying it's clear we've had a relationship, DJ."

"What? Yeah, we worked that one job together, but that don't mean nothin'."

Charity smiled at Paul. "DJ and I had a little fling. So what?"

DJ's mouth curled into a crooked grin. "Now, I wouldn't characterize it *that* way."

Paul held up his hands. "That's neither here nor there to me."

"Right. And you still haven't answered my question. Why are you really here?"

"I told you. When—"

Charity held up a hand. "You know what? Just forget it. I know

I'm not going to get a straight answer."

"Charity, you seem to think I have an agenda. I assure you, I do not."

"No offense, but you're a shrink, right? I mean, an agenda always comes with the territory."

"If you mean I'm prone to want to help people, even those who don't want it—well, yes, I suppose it does."

Charity glanced at her watch. Had they only been there for twenty minutes? "I need some air," she said and headed for the door.

"Good idea," Paul said, and followed her out.

The sun was barely above the western rim of the shallow valley. Charity looked toward it, always attracted by the red and orange hues it cast on everything at that time of day—the golden hour.

She turned and headed back toward the other building. Another pass through it might turn up something.

Paul followed her.

She didn't need his intrusion. Nor did Savannah.

She took her phone out and muted her microphone as she rounded the corner.

"You know, a lot of people benefit from talk therapy," Paul said behind her. "That's why it's usually required in situations like this."

She spun on him. "What the hell is this? You, of all people, know my history, know what I've done, what I'm capable of, and what I've overcome and accomplished."

"Charity," he said, attempting that soothing voice. "You just killed a man. A fact you haven't even acknowledged yet."

She smirked. "Are you fucking kidding me? I've killed dozens of men. And you know it. You think I'm bothered by one more cartel thug being dragged down to the depths of Hell by my bullet? I don't think so. Besides, even if I did want to talk, which I *don't*, this isn't the time or the place to have this conversation. You're a trained operator, so I know you know that, too."

"What did you feel when you shot that man and ended his life?" Paul demanded, getting straight to the point.

Charity strode toward him and looked him in the eye, hers shifting left and right from one of his to the other, their faces inches apart.

"You want to know what I *felt* when I killed him?"

"Yes, I do," he replied calmly.

"Recoil," she replied flatly, then started to turn away from him.

Paul grabbed her arm. "I can't help you if you're not willing to help yourself."

She stopped and looked at his hand on her arm, letting her gaze rise to meet his.

He released her arm.

"Is that a line they teach you people in shrink school?" she asked. "Because I've heard it before. Your presence is only complicating things. I'm still not sure why you're here."

"As I said, Armstrong—"

"Yes," she nodded. "When Jack or Colonel Stockwell summons, you jump."

"To this day, you still call him by the rank he hasn't held in decades."

"It's an Army thing. You wouldn't get it."

She turned and continued on her way.

"I'm simply concerned about you," he said to her back.

"Don't be," she shot over her shoulder.

"But I care about you," he said, again following after her. "And it's my job."

Charity spun back around again. "I knew it. Stockwell sent you to evaluate me, didn't he? Why? What have I done to prompt that?"

Paul gave no reaction. "Are you asking if you *deserve* to have someone concerned about your well-being?"

Charity knew this conversation was a trap. She smiled to disarm him. "You're right. I'm sorry."

"Even you can see that you're wound up pretty tight."

"Okay, I admit that." *Just keep appeasing him.*

"And I think it's fair to assume you're concerned about Savannah."

"What? No. I mean, yes. Of course. She..."

"She's not like you. She's upset, struggling with her decision to give the order."

"Exactly," Charity said.

He said nothing, simply stared, waiting.

Was this about Savannah? Had Armstrong known all about what happened between the three of them that night on Jesse's boat?

Chyrel certainly did. Had she included that in her report? Did Jack or Stockwell purposefully put Savannah in a position to test her? What the hell was going on?

Finally, she said, "We still haven't located the subject."

"The subject?"

"The girl, Paul. Harper Landry. We made a lot of noise here and have nothing to show for it. Worse, we might've blown the whole thing. They took that proof-of-life picture with us in the background for a reason. So, yeah, if I were in Savvy's shoes, I'd be worried. This op's gone to shit. She's gonna have to pull a rabbit out of a hat now."

"She'll need your help."

Charity looked into Paul's eyes, carefully thinking about a response.

Before she came up with one, he continued, "It's a good thing

195

you happened to be here."

"I didn't *happen* to be here. I was trying to find her."

A slight sparkle came to his eyes and Charity could swear that one corner of his mouth moved upward just a little.

"Why?" he asked. "She's a capable, adult woman who left her husband. Why were you so concerned that you took it upon yourself to track her down?"

"So, this inquiry is about that, then?"

"Charity, there's no inquiry."

"Seems like it."

"Do you always feel like you have to live full-time on the defensive?"

She crossed her arms. "What does that even mean?"

"It means that I'm concerned that you're not yourself. I can sense that you're worried about something. Maybe it's Savannah. I feel there's some deep emotions going on between..." He trailed off, his shocked eyes going to Charity's shirt pocket as his mouth fell open.

Charity grinned at his discomfort.

"I muted my phone when I came out."

Paul quickly gathered himself. "There's a problem between you two," he said. "Or maybe it's something else entirely. But I don't think so. What I'm trying to tell you is that I'm here to help. And, for the record, when it comes to a firefight, I can guarantee the situation would be better if I were armed and not your driver."

Charity stared at him for a long moment. "You can help by staying out of my way."

He frowned.

"And out of my head."

She spun around and left him, then immediately realized he was right, at least about the distribution of firepower. She'd felt Enrique had the heart of a fighter when they'd first met, and he had far more reason to fight than Paul. But she didn't know how he'd react in a firefight, if it came to one.

Years earlier, Jesse had trained all of Deuce's DHS team in marksmanship. They'd used a wide assortment of rifles, handguns, even grenade launchers, sending tens of thousands of rounds of ammunition downrange.

Jesse had been not only familiar with every weapon Deuce produced, but had proven to be very competent with each one. But he was a master with the long gun.

Second to him, in regard to familiarity with a wide variety of weapons, had been Paul Bender, the quiet Secret Service agent who'd earned a PhD in forensic psychology. He'd said at the time that he'd trained his presidential detail with every gun the federal government had access to, thinking that in the event of an overthrow, weapons of chance would be needed when an agent ran out of ammo.

So, without any reservation, Charity intended to remedy that problem. Enrique would understand. He wouldn't like it, but she was sure he'd accept it if she asked. After all, it was an M-1 Carbine, probably the most manufactured rifle ever made. She knew Paul would be at least as proficient with it as Enrique.

When she entered the barn, she noted it was big enough for a tractor but had probably been built with a horse and wagon in mind.

She couldn't quite determine the original purpose of the two buildings; the smaller one couldn't even be called a casita, which Charity had always equated to a quaint little AirBnB she'd once stayed at on the beach up in Tampico.

"Probably a horse barn at one time," she said, working her way around the room to the left side. "What anyone would farm out here is another story."

There was a pile of empty bottles with no labels—more proof that the stench was from homemade tequila.

A moonshiner's camp?

"It wouldn't be a very good idea to light a match in here," Paul said.

He was right. The liquor smell permeated the air, but she could also smell gasoline. Then there were the cans on the shelves. No telling what was in those.

A filthy and torn tan sleeping bag lay rumpled in a corner where moldy straw was piled up. It looked as if someone had just gotten up from it and then tossed some hay over it.

Charity hadn't noticed it on her first quick inspection, covered with hay like it was. Perhaps she'd been concentrating on finding something that made her think she saw a gray van and had overlooked this corner.

Had this been where they'd forced Harper to sit and wait?

She kicked the corner, folding it partly back upon itself. Charity grimaced in the gathering gloom as Paul came closer.

Then she noticed a slat in the wall was askew. She moved it aside and grinned, realizing this definitely was *not* where Harper had rested.

Reaching in, she pulled out a Sig Sauer P229. She turned toward Paul, making an instantaneous decision. She knew the weapon she'd just found was long standard with the Secret Service.

She thrust it toward him, butt first. "You're right. I don't know how good Enrique is with that old carbine of his, but I'd bet he's better with it than a gun he doesn't know."

Paul took the Sig and press checked the slide, then racked it, chambering a round. "A 229's no good without a round in the chamber. Now what about DJ?"

"We had a fling," she reaffirmed, then decided to push back and make *him* feel uncomfortable. "The truth is, I screwed his brains out and left him babbling incoherently."

Paul's eyebrow arched slightly. "I meant what about arming *him* instead of Enrique."

CHAPTER TWENTY-FOUR

Back in the small house, Charity distanced herself from Paul, telling DJ that she was going to rest. The ad hoc team would fall into a watch routine—inside and out—without having to assign anyone. DJ was standing at the door, looking through a crack, while Enrique slept in a corner.

Paul took the hint and sat next to the fisherman, closing his eyes as he leaned against the wall.

Though he was a shrink, Charity knew that he was also a very capable field operative and would know to rest whenever possible.

There was always an unseen enemy out there, Charity thought, *constantly expending energy, searching for her.*

She needed the rest, and pretended to do just that, closing her eyes to give her time to think about Paul's questions and if he was really there as an operative, or was sent to analyze her.

She leaned back against the inside of the rough planks of the exterior wall and tilted her head and shoulder against one of the bare studs. Her eyes were closed, not meaning to fall asleep. But soon, as the others talked occasionally in whispers, her mind drifted....

Charity rose from the forward-facing bench seat on the flybridge of *Gaspar's Revenge*. She moved to the front rail, letting the robe fall to her feet. She stood there, looking out over the Sea of Abaco toward Marsh Harbor, thinking back on what had transpired.

Ending the lives of two men who needed it didn't really bother her all that much. It did at first, but over the last fifteen years, Charity had dispatched more than forty souls to an eternity in Hell. They haunted her dreams, but those nightmares were coming less frequently.

A foreign emotion held Charity's thoughts as she gazed up at the stars, one that she hadn't felt in ages, and which made her feel uncomfortable even under just the starlight. She subconsciously took a tiny step back from the rail.

Her quick thinking and very awkward distraction had probably kept the police from boarding. She *knew* that. But something deep in her subconscious was struggling with what had happened.

The adrenaline from the encounter with the two men on the beach, then the hard swim back, coupled with the *way* she'd distracted the police had subsided even before Jesse had come up to check on her.

Her first thoughts after experiencing something like they'd gone through always turned to her father, her uncle, then the men she'd loved and lost, almost always to violence.

All gone now.

When she looked at the open hatch on the foredeck, knowing that Jesse was lying there, she suddenly felt *shame,* an emotion that she hadn't experienced in many years.

What she'd done had *worked*. It was the most logical move to have made.

So, why did she feel shame?

202

She suddenly saw the scene play out from a bird's-eye view—from Savannah's view, as she watched on the computer screen.

Charity bowed her head and began to cry, taking another step back. She felt the rope at her feet, turned and picked it up, shrugging it back on, though the night air was warm.

Sitting alone with her thoughts, she put her face in her hands and wept.

"Charity," a woman's voice whispered in an urgent tone. "Charity, wake up."

Charity sat bolt upright, shifting her butt back to the wall she'd dozed off against. Poppy was kneeling beside her.

Charity blinked, instantly alert and fully aware. "Sit-rep," she said, then realized Poppy wasn't prior military and might not understand her request for a situation report. "What's going on?"

"Our eyes in the sky spotted a car stop at the park entrance," Poppy replied, looking at her with an odd expression.

"Then it turned down our trail and parked," DJ added, looking through a narrow crack in the door.

He had Enrique's rifle.

Charity rose, picked up her own rifle, and quickly crossed the dirt floor to stand close beside DJ. "See anything yet?"

"One man," Savannah announced, her calm voice emanating from DJ's shirt pocket. "He went on foot back up to the parking lot and is looking at Enrique's van."

"We're in position, Savannah," Charity heard Paul's voice say.

Charity turned. The fisherman was sitting alone, leaning against the wall, but awake.

203

"Savannah sent Paul and Kevin over to the rocks, just across from us," DJ informed her.

Charity took her own phone out of her pocket and turned the volume up slightly before dropping it back in and buttoning the pocket.

"How'd you end up with Enrique's rifle?" she whispered.

DJ turned his head, their faces just inches apart. "I asked if he'd ever shot a man and he just up and handed it to me."

"Probably thought it matched the hardware on your leg," she chided.

"Hoo-ah," he grunted quietly, turning back to the door.

"Airborne leads the way," she whispered back.

Though they never served together, Charity and DJ shared a bond from long before the night in they'd shared their darkest thoughts and had then shared their bodies.

They were both Army Airborne. Though DJ was an infantryman and she a pilot, they knew they could count on one another under any circumstance.

"The person is moving down the trail again," Savannah said. "Passing his car and still headed down the trail. Walks like a man and is wearing a hat. He doesn't appear to be armed. At least not openly."

Though Charity knew she had to be exhausted, Savannah sounded confident again—large and in charge, just like Jesse.

"Only a single heat signature," Chyrel added. "Whoever it is, he's alone."

Charity ducked under DJ's arm and squirmed between him and the door to peer through the crack below him.

"Where're Paul and Kevin?" she asked, relieved to hear that Savannah seemed to be in full control once more.

204

"At two o'clock," DJ replied. "From the front porch, that is."

In the distance, Charity saw Paul step from behind a large rock into the moonlight. "To get to you," he said, "they have to walk past us."

"He's halfway down," Savannah said. "Suggest you go quiet, interpret his behavior, and act accordingly. If he even hints at being shady, take him alive for information."

"And if he doesn't want to give it up?" Charity asked.

"Make him," came Savannah's firm response. "We have to find Harper. Time's running out. Damn!"

"What's wrong?"

"That Sergeant Quintero is coming back," Savannah replied. "He is most definitely not a nice man."

"I didn't meet him," Charity said.

"Count your blessings. I'll get rid of him as quickly as I can. Y'all be careful."

"Roger that."

The seconds ticked by. After an eternity, Savannah was back and said that they should be able to put eyes on the intruder in just another minute.

Finally, Charity saw someone moving down the left rut of the trail toward them.

He was advancing cautiously, quietly picking his way over loose stones. Finally, he stepped away from a large bush, halfway between Paul and Kevin's position and the front porch.

The man started waving his arms over his head. "*Hola, Santiago! Soy yo Filipe!*"

"It is a cartel man," the fisherman whispered in Spanish. "He is calling for the man you killed."

"Answer him," Charity responded accordingly. "Tell him

Santiago went off to look around. Tell him to come into the house."

The fisherman grumbled his lines as if he were tired and irritated, which he was.

"*Por qué estás ahí?*" the newcomer asked, his voice sounding suspicious.

"Swarm him!" Savannah ordered. "Now!"

Without hesitation, DJ flung the door open, leading with the old carbine. He went left and Charity went right, advancing in a crouch, weapons trained on the newcomer.

"*No se mueva!*" Paul shouted, as he and Kevin came charging out of the rocks.

"*Manos arriba,*" Charity ordered, as the four surrounded the man.

He instantly raised both hands high over his head.

Poppy came out and strode straight toward him, an air of confidence about her.

She stopped in front of the man. "*Eres* Felipe Pérez. *Correcto?*"

Behind the man, Kevin was making a rolling motion with his hands. Charity took that to mean "roll with it."

Poppy knew his name.

The man's shoulders seemed to tighten, and his eyes grew wide as he stared at Agent McVie. "You know my name?" he asked, in accented English, then paused. "I do nothing wrong."

"So if I check your car, I won't find any *turtles*?" Poppy snapped.

"Car? No." He shook his head so hard his hat fell to the ground. He made no effort to retrieve it. "I no have car. I walk here."

"And the car you left five hundred meters up the hill?"

"A green 1994 Ford F-150," Savannah's voice said from all four cell phones, surprising the man. "Base XL model, four-wheel drive."

He shook his head again, but his shoulders slumped in defeat.

Poppy continued. "Are you with the South Pacific Cartel now?"

"No, no, no." Pérez whined. "You no understand."

"This is a known location used by the cartel. You're telling me you just happened to be hiking by, and calling out for Santiago?"

"We are friends. Just friends."

Poppy stepped toward him, and he seemed to shrink. Charity didn't think she had that kind of presence, but this man sure responded to her. He was putty in her hands.

"*Por favor, señora.* No jail," Filipe begged. "*Tengo una familia.*"

"And why should your having a family matter to me?" Poppy said.

"*No sé.* No jail! *Por favor!* Tell me and I do. Whatever you say, *señora.*"

"You can start by telling me where else these men might be. They must have other locations like this one, where you meet them."

"*Si.* Yes. One ..." He pointed over the hill to the north. "*Justo sobre esa colina.*"

"Yes, we know about that one," Poppy told him. "You're going to have to do a little better."

"*Si, si,*" Filipe said excitedly. "Another. *Una casa*—a house—*ocho kilómetros desde aquí.*"

"I need details."

Filipe was more than willing to give up the third location rather than go to jail.

"I've got it," Savannah said over the phone. "And what appears to be a gray cargo van is parked under some sort of carport or overhang."

"Let's move," Charity said to the team.

Poppy marched the man into the house, bound his wrists, and

left him with the fisherman.

When they reached the top of the hill where Filipe had left his pickup, Poppy veered toward it and looked inside.

"What is it?" Charity asked, as Poppy opened the passenger door.

She reached inside and took a large burlap bag out of the floor of the truck. Upending it gently on the ground, she emptied the bag of its contents.

"Turtles," Poppy replied, as more than a dozen small box turtles scurried down the hill.

When they reached Enrique's van, Savannah's voice came over the phone in Charity's pocket. "There's something y'all need to know."

"What is it?" Charity asked, standing by the front passenger door.

"Sergeant Quintero just left," Savannah began. "He was very adamant about our snooping around."

"How could he possibly know?" DJ asked, standing next to Charity.

"He knew about the meeting with Rosita Gonzales," Savannah replied, her voice catching a little. "She was shot and killed less than an hour ago."

CHAPTER TWENTY-FIVE

They rode in silence for several minutes. DJ sat in back, his face a mask as to exactly what he was thinking, but Charity could tell he was in a dark place.

Rosita was killed because she'd talked to them; Charity was sure of it.

She was still trying to figure out who the proof-of-life photo was supposed to include. It was obviously meant to be a threat.

Rosita Gonzales had been in the picture, and now she was dead. Charity had been too consumed by finding Harper and, if she were honest, distracted by her concerns about Savannah, to ask for protection for the woman. That was on her. But she also knew that DJ had been aware of the danger as well. He'd made first contact with Rosita and seemed to have a personal connection. More than his usual, anyway. He'd have a hard time with this one.

But why send a picture of Rosita? Why not just kill her?

The *logical* assumption was that they'd meant to include Jojo in the picture, since they knew he was working with the judge as a negotiator. But something didn't feel right about that either. She'd tried in the past to find out about him and gotten nowhere. She doubted the cartel was able to dig up information that she hadn't that quickly.

Someone could have been surveilling the *MollySue* after the kidnapping. That's what she would do. But did they have that kind of network in place?

And just how were the turtle smugglers a part of anything? Could Poppy's case really be the tie-in to all this? It was too big of a coincidence that a man had shown up with a bag of turtles.

"It's almost midnight," Savannah said, her voice coming over everyone's phone as Enrique drove away from the park. "It's been nearly twenty-four hours."

None of them needed to be reminded. One day was about the limit a kidnapping investigation had.

Typically, if a hostage wasn't rescued within the first twenty-four hours, the chance of a positive resolution diminished greatly. Keeping the kidnap victim alive any longer was risky.

"How did you know that guy?" DJ asked Poppy from the back, his voice low and sullen.

Charity could tell he was trying to move his mind away from his dark thoughts, away from Rosita, and he was mulling over the same questions she was.

"Before we flew down," Poppy whispered. "Kevin and I went over some local suspects. When he said his name, I thought it couldn't be, but then I recognized him right away. He's a known buncher in the area."

"A buncher?" DJ asked, sitting forward from the rear seat, his broad shoulders cramming the gap between the two middle-row seats.

"Think of him as a middleman in turtle smuggling," Poppy explained. "He buys from the poachers, tends to the inventory, then sells to the smuggling kingpin, who in this case, I'm guessing, was Santiago. We'll have to follow up, but I think *we* just got lucky."

"Lucky, indeed," Paul said. "He didn't seem like he'd be a very cooperative interrogee at first, but he was definitely intimidated by your presence. Good work."

Almost as if he knew her, Charity thought, *or knew what she looked like, but they'd never met.*

"Charity woulda got him talkin'," DJ said. "It might've taken a few minutes longer, but pain's a great motivator."

Charity caught Paul's reaction as he looked disapprovingly at her in the front seat.

She didn't care. She'd used pain, even extreme pain, to get answers from people before. Call it persuasion. Call it torture. It didn't matter. Was it really all that bad to do the same thing to some degenerate that he had likely done to a long list of others?

Not in Charity's mind. Two kicks to the *cojones* was usually all any man could stand. And with a big ape like DJ holding the little cartel thug upright, she could have done it over and over and never broken a sweat.

What's more, she'd get answers.

"How long till we get there?" she asked Enrique.

"Not long," he replied. "It is just on the outskirts of town. About ten minutes."

They rode in silence for another mile. Then Enrique looked over at Charity as he slowed for a traffic circle.

"These men are few in numbers," he said. "But they have many guns, which frighten the people, and a lot of cash that even the most pious cannot resist. They have bribed most of the police, and the people are too afraid to speak. Do not expect help from anyone. Some might even join the cartel in the fight."

"Then they make themselves targets," Charity said, then glanced back at the others. "We go in fast and hard. Shoot anyone that isn't a scared young American college girl. If any one of us hesitates, we could all die."

She got a nod from everyone in the back.

"Does that work for you, Savvy?" she asked.

"Be hyperalert when you go in," Savannah replied, her voice firm. "We don't want Harper to be hurt accidentally."

Charity had Enrique pull over several hundred feet from the target house and on the opposite side of the road.

"What do you guys see, Savvy?"

"The satellite is looking down at about twenty degrees still," Savannah replied. "The east, west, and south sides of the house are clear, and the gray van parked in the carport looks a lot like you described, Charity."

"I'm getting only three heat signatures inside the house," Chyrel said. "Looks like one large and one small person in the front room, likely to the right of the front door and against the front wall. There's a single small heat source in the back room. The van in the driveway is as cold as the ground."

That meant that whoever had arrived in the van had been there for at least an hour or two; otherwise, the van's engine would still show residual heat. It also meant they'd likely be moving soon,

"DJ," Charity said, turning in her seat, "how's Patty?"

He'd named his prosthetic "Patty O'Doure" for some odd reason that only made sense to DJ.

He looked up at her and grinned. "Patty three-point-oh," he said. "Newer and stronger foot."

Charity smiled back. "You're the designated door kicker, then. Switch guns with Poppy."

DJ glanced at Enrique's M-1, which he was leaning on. "You sure?"

"I'm sure she's better with a rifle than you," Charity said. "And I know you can go through a door better than anyone else here. If you fall after breaching, a handgun will be easier for you to bring into action."

"I'll go second," Paul said. "Right behind DJ, to cover any sector he doesn't."

"My rifle's shorter," Charity said to Poppy. "Kevin and I will breach together and hopefully not trip over DJ and Paul. You'll bring up the rear and make sure nobody outside comes in."

Poppy nodded and exchanged weapons with DJ.

Charity leaned forward and looked upward through the van's windshield. "We have a bright full moon almost directly overhead." Then she studied the house for a moment. "The sidewalk from the curb is clear for a running start, DJ. Any change in the heat signatures, Chyrel?"

"Not even the slightest movement," Chyrel replied. "I'm also not getting any tiny spot signatures from lights. They might be asleep."

"If they are," Savannah said, "and we can take them by total surprise, we'll take them alive."

It was the same stance she'd taken with Paladin and Cordova. Only then, Savannah hadn't been privy to the phone call Paladin had made, promising to kill more innocent people.

But now?

Charity bristled. "When it comes to the life of an innocent young woman and the life of a cartel turd fondler—"

"I know, Charity," Savannah said, her voice calm. "And I agree with you. But if it's at all possible... Well, let's not make it any messier than we have to."

"We can only react to the situation as it unfolds," DJ said from

213

the back, his head down again, and his body rocking back and forth.

Charity knew what he was doing—psyching himself for battle. "The plan is always the first casualty after contact with the enemy." He sighed. "I ain't makin' no promises, Savvy, but quarter will be given. Until one of 'em pulls a gun or knife. Then, it's 'Katy bar the door.'"

"Roger that," Savannah said. "That's all I ask. Be careful."

"We go in with phones at full volume," Charity ordered. "Loud and disruptive, with overwhelming force. We neutralize the two in front, then DJ and Paul move to the third person in the back room, clearing any other rooms as you go. Doesn't matter if they hear instructions from our phones at this point. This whole thing will be over in less than sixty seconds. They won't have time to react. At most there are three people inside and it's likely the two right by the entry will be the only tangos."

"Poppy," Kevin said, "move over here and flip that seat up. Then you lead the way and get flat against the wall. I'll follow you and do the same. If anything happens, we can cover DJ as he runs for the door with Paul behind him."

"Good plan," DJ said, palming Charity's ultra-slim handgun in his big fist. "Enrique, you stay with the van, *amigo*. Be ready when we come out with Harper."

Poppy folded the back of her seat down, then flipped the whole thing forward into the footwell, allowing maximum exit room on that side.

"Okay, Enrique," Charity said, taking a deep breath. "Pull up to the driveway and stop right behind the van."

Enrique started the engine, but left the headlights turned off. The moon was more than bright enough.

As he pulled to the curb in front of the house and stopped,

Savannah's voice came over their phones. "All clear on the street. No movement inside. Go! Go!"

Instantly, Poppy slid the door back as Charity threw open the front passenger door and charged around the hood of the van with her bullpup rifle. She stopped and covered the street for a moment as Poppy and Kevin moved quickly up the sidewalk, then she fell in behind Paul as they all ran up the steps and onto the porch.

Poppy moved to the left side of the door, back against the wall, carbine ready, as Kevin moved into a similar position on the opposite side.

DJ didn't slow at all, taking the first step with his prosthetic, then planting his good foot on the porch, and launching Patty at a spot above the doorknob, kicking downward very hard.

Wood splintered and the door gave way, crashing into an interior wall, perpendicular to the front wall of the house.

DJ followed the door, rolling forward and coming up in a shooting stance, covering the uncleared sector to the right of the entry.

Paul was right behind DJ, covering the forward sector, aiming down a short hallway over DJ's head.

Charity saw all of this, her senses hyperaware once more, as she came through the door, Kevin right beside her.

The DB9 in DJ's hand boomed at the same instant he shouted, "Gun!"

Paul turned and fired also, as Charity brought her rifle to bear on two men with guns, one in a chair and the other on a couch, both with blood already soaking the fronts of their shirts.

Suddenly, one of the dead men moved, and Charity recognized the snake and crocodile tattoos of a third man as he came up off the couch from behind one of the dead men, a sawed-off shotgun swinging toward DJ.

Charity fired and the crack of her rifle was joined by three more shots.

The tattooed man's body was slammed against the far wall from the impact of four bullets to his chest.

Apparently the two men on the couch had looked like a single heat signature to Chyrel.

"Three armed tangos down," Charity said.

A high-pitched scream came from the back of the house, and DJ moved quickly down the hall, Paul right behind him.

With Kevin covering, Charity checked the three men.

They were all dead.

Suddenly, Paul reappeared. "DJ's got Harper! Let's get the hell out of here!"

CHAPTER TWENTY-SIX

Enrique mashed the accelerator to the floor, then turned on the headlights as they headed north into Campeche, the narrow streets swallowing them quickly.

"Take it easy," Charity cautioned him, looking back through the van's rear window. "We're good. Nobody's following us."

Enrique slowed, and Charity looked down at Harper, on the floor between DJ and Paul in the middle row.

"Are you okay, Harper?"

"Who... who are you?" Then recognition dawned on her. She sat upright and shrank back. "But you're Savannah's friend. What's going on?"

DJ turned away from the window and smiled at the girl. "It's okay. We're all friends of Savannah and Alberto."

"Are you hurt?" Charity asked, taking a bottle of water from Enrique's cooler between the seats, and handing it to her.

Harper tried to take the bottle, struggling with her hands still tied.

"Here, let me help you with that," Paul said, taking a locking knife from a pouch on his belt and clicking it open. He quickly parted the ropes that bound her.

"Friend's of Savannah?" she asked, still disoriented and

confused, though she accepted the bottle and turned it up to her mouth.

"They are," Kevin said from the back. "Poppy and I only just met her today." He took his phone from his pocket and handed it to the girl. "Here. She's on the line now and your mom is right there with her."

Harper took the phone and put it to her ear, sobbing. "Mom?"

Her voice echoed in the van, coming from everyone else's phones as well, and startling her.

"Savannah?" Harper asked, nervously. "Is anyone there?" She looked up at Kevin. "There's nobody there."

Then she noticed Poppy and fixed her gaze on her. "You have red hair," she murmured. "Red hair. It must have been red hair."

"What are you talking about?" Charity asked. "Does that mean something?"

"I thought they were talking about a red horse."

"A red horse?" she asked, as Enrique turned and headed toward the pier.

"I overheard them talking," Harper replied. "They thought I didn't know any Spanish, so I was able to pick up a few things. They moved me a lot—several different places—always moving. This morning, someone called and told the tattooed guy something that made him angry. He got another call just a few minutes later and he nearly flipped out. They put me in the van and drove around all morning. I thought they said they were looking for a red horse and were going to kill it, but horse and hair sound a lot alike in Spanish."

Charity nodded. "*Cabello rojo* and *caballo rojo*, easy mistake."

"We drove around most of the morning. Finally, they opened the door of the van and made me sit in front of it while the tattooed guy took a picture." She turned and looked at Poppy. "They must

218

have been looking for you. *El cabello rojo.*"

"The proof-of-life photo," Charity said with a sigh, then looked up at Poppy. "It was you. They were killing two birds with one stone. Proof of life and a direct threat toward you. They must've been alerted by corrupt authorities when you entered the country. You've got a bounty on your head by the cartel."

"I don't understand," said Harper. "Were they after you instead of me?"

Charity turned her attention back to Poppy. "I don't think you're safe in Mexico."

"She's right!" Harper exclaimed. "After they took the picture, they blindfolded me again and took me to a smelly old shack and the tattooed man called someone and told him to find and kill the red horse. Someone's going to try to kill you!"

"It's okay," DJ said in a soothing tone, placing his hand softly on her shoulder. "He already tried and my partner, Charity, stopped the guy. It doesn't matter. You're safe now. We're all safe."

"Charity?" Harper asked looking up at her. "I thought you said your name was Gabby."

"That's my cover," Charity replied. "I work for DHS."

"What happened after the tattooed man made the call?" Paul asked, his voice calm as always.

Harper looked up at him. "Then we took off again, and they drove to that place you found me. They started drinking and laughing about the red horse their man was going to kill. I was locked in a room, but I could hear them snoring for at least an hour before you got there and..."

"Got you out safely," Poppy said, enunciating each word as she leaned forward and stroked the girl's hair. "That's all you need to concentrate on, okay? You're safe now. Don't worry about me."

"That's right," Paul agreed. "You've been through a terrible ordeal and you're safe now. That's all you need to concern yourself with tonight. In just a few minutes, you'll be back with your mom and shortly after that, home and safe."

"Is Harper all right?" Savannah's urgent voice came from every phone.

"Yes!" Harper shouted. "I'm okay! Thank you, Savannah! Whatever you did, thank you! Is my mom with you?"

Charity took her phone out and disconnected from the call, nodding at the others to do the same, so Harper and her mother could talk privately.

"What happened to you, Savvy?" DJ asked, before he disconnected. "You disappeared from the com again."

"As soon as Charity said the cartel men were down, I went to get Suzette. Here she is now, Harper."

"Baby?" Suzette's voice came over Kevin's speaker as DJ disconnected.

Kevin took his phone from Harper, turned the speaker off, then returned it to her.

"Mom!" she squealed, putting the phone to her ear. "I'm here, Mom! I can see the pier ahead!"

Charity looked around at the others, all watching the young girl and smiling.

She was safe—her ordeal finally over.

She glanced over at Enrique, who had a tear running down his cheek. He glanced at her and smiled. "*Viva la gente libre.*"

"Long live the free people," Charity agreed. Then she looked ahead toward the long pier. "The head's been cut off the snake, Enrique," she said softly. "And the crocodile, too, I suppose. It will be up to you and the people of Campeche to keep the serpent from growing another head."

Enrique parked in his usual spot, and everyone piled out of the van, all weapons carefully concealed inside Charity's camera case, except Enrique's.

The customs guard at the gate barely paid any attention to the group of gringo cruisers, and they quickly climbed down to the waiting tender.

As they motored out, with Paul at the helm, Charity sat next to Harper on the small bench, forward of the helm. Harper had her nose buried in Kevin's phone. Ahead of them, Kevin stood in the bow, scanning the water for any boat traffic.

Charity looked back and noticed DJ in the stern, watching for any following threat. Poppy sat near him, also clicking away on her phone like Harper.

Charity breathed a deep sigh of relief just as her phone chirped an incoming message. She looked down at it as Paul turned toward *MollySue*, anchored in a pool of her own bright lights.

The text was from Savannah.

Tired and taking Alberto back to Sea Biscuit. *We'll catch up in the morning. Please arrange to get everyone home for me.*

Catch up? What the hell? They'd just gotten Harper back. They had to debrief. Arrangements had to be made for the others to get back home, or to wherever they came from. She and Savannah still needed to talk about what had happened between her and Jesse.

Charity started to text her back, but realized that Savannah had likely spent the whole previous night awake at the helm, returning to Campeche. Not to mention the obvious emotional turmoil she'd been under.

Okay, she typed back, then hit the *Send* button.

I can handle making any arrangements that needed to be made, she

221

thought. The priority should be toward getting Harper and Suzette back to New Orleans as soon as possible.

"I can get us on a ten o'clock to DFW," Poppy said to Kevin. "Back to New Orleans by this evening."

DJ looked up, grinning. "N'awlins? How ya tryin' to get there?"

"Commercial," Poppy replied, then looked back at Kevin. "That's the earliest."

DJ looked over at Charity. "I think they've been a great asset," he said. "And us working with other agencies is always a good thing. Ain't that what Mr. Armstrong always says? N'awlins ain't much out of our way."

"You have a plane?" Poppy asked, surprised.

Charity nodded at DJ.

"Not just any old plane," DJ said, checking his watch. "In fact, if you two agree to buy the first round, I think we can get ya to Lafitte's Blacksmith Bar before last call."

"I thought you were going back to Florida," Charity said.

"Not if our new friends need a lift," DJ replied. "That'd just be rude." Then his eyes sparkled. "Hey, we should all go. The G-550 can get us there by three, easy. And N'awlins never sleeps."

"I have to meet with Savannah in the morning," Charity said, trying to concentrate on just the next step in front of her. "We have to... uh... debrief and all that."

"Think she'd mind if the plane goes to N'awlins?" DJ asked. "On its way to Fort Meade, I mean, instead of stoppin' in Florida?"

"How will you get home?" Charity asked.

Kevin leaned closer as Paul turned the boat toward *MollySue's* stern. "I'm sure the Alliance would cover that in exchange for a ride back for the two of us."

"It's settled then," DJ said to Charity. "We're all buggin' out, except for you and Savvy, savvy?"

She smiled at him and nodded.

When the tender pulled up to *MollySue's* swim platform, Suzette and Jojo were there waiting.

"Harper!" she called.

The girl climbed over the side of the boat and fell into her mother's arms.

"Grab your gear, Jojo," DJ said. "Our plane leaves in thirty minutes."

Charity made an instant decision, though she too was very tired. "Suzette, you should have the captain leave here as soon as possible," she said. "We have a plane on standby, arriving in New Orleans tonight. Grab what you and Harper need, and you'll be in your own beds before the sun comes up."

Charity knew that by morning, they'd be home safe, and she'd be facing Savannah, the reason she'd come in the first place. Maybe, after rescuing Harper, Savannah would be feeling optimistic and forgiving.

She hoped.

CHAPTER TWENTY-SEVEN

It was very early when the jailer had roused the man from bed. And it was the Fourth of July—Independence Day. At least he thought it was. He'd kinda lost track of time.

The morning sunlight streaming in through the windows made the nearly empty courtroom seem warm and bright, unlike the dingy cell he'd been in for over two weeks.

Didn't matter, Marcus thought. Life was pickin' up. Yeah, it was Independence Day all right, whether it was the fourth or not. He'd be outta here by the afternoon.

JP had gotten word to him that everything was taken care of, he didn't need to worry about nothin'. The boss had everything handled, and he just had to be patient.

Patience was one thing. What he needed was a beer and a New York strip, charred to perfection and slathered with A-1. He could taste it already, hot off his backyard grill, sizzlin' away. He'd make some baked potatoes and stuff them with cheese and sour cream. Maybe even get some of them chives to sprinkle on top. And bacon.

Then he'd set off some fireworks. Not the cheap ones, but the ones that made a big bang and lots of sparklin' colors. He'd loved that shit ever since he was a kid. His uncle and he would get a whole box of 'em—cherry bombs, silver salutes, M-1000 half sticks, roman candles—and they'd set 'em off on the dock.

His mom always nagged about people losin' their fingers and shit. But he wasn't a dumbass like that. He knew what he was doin'. He was the man. He'd set off fireworks if he damn well wanted to. A whole box of 'em. Just like when he was a kid. He'd get 'em all. He especially liked the ones that shot up fireballs, one right after another, makin' a loud bang each time. That's the kind he would find for tonight.

Yeah, that's what he was goin' to do. Celebrate.

But before that, he was goin' to stretch out in the lounge chair and watch the sun set. After a couple of weeks in the slammer, he missed the sun.

Besides that, it hadn't been much of a hassle, really. He was plugged in and people knew him. Maybe he didn't have the muscle some had, but he had connections, and that meant a whole lot more in the parrish joint. In here or out there, he was the man. When he said jump, people jumped. As high as he wanted.

Whoever had ratted on him and got him into this shit was gator bait. It wouldn't take him long to figure it out. He had eyes everywhere. Even inside. Damn rats with their collusion, or whatever it was called. They didn't follow the code.

And they'd pay for it.

He just had to be patient.

He sat in the front row by himself. There was no one else in the courtroom, except for the staff, which was minimal. He was pretty sure it was Tuesday, the fourth. But it being a four-day weekend, it might be any one of those days, to have so few staff on hand.

It was a special day. A special case. The judge was gonna let him go, and the fewer there were around, the better it'd be for his rep.

That was odd, but he figured most of the court employees were

226

off for the holiday. That's how it was when you worked for the man. You got told when you could come and go.

Too bad for these saps.

They were here on their day off to set him free. Seemed fittin', seein's how they'd put him in here for no good cause. Sons-a-bitches thought they knew who was in charge.

They were like sheep, all talk about law and order and shit. They had no idea. He was the man. They'd see.

The cop said for everyone to rise, so he got to his feet. Why make waves now? He'd declined a lawyer, because a public defender might expect him to tell him his business, and he wasn't about to do that. That's how they got you. Acted like they were there to help, then before you knew it, bam, you were back in the clink. Well, he wasn't that stupid.

The judge strolled in, all high and mighty in his black robe. He sat down on his throne and his eyes fell on Marcus.

Somethin' wasn't right.

Marcus shifted uncomfortably in his chair.

Hadn't he been paid off or somethin'? JP had assured him....

But this judge looked pissed.

His nerves started to buzz.

"The honorable Judge Landry presiding," someone announced.

There was some other jibber-jabber about docket numbers and such. Then his name was called.

Odd, since he was the only one there. They sure had their rules about how stuff was supposed to be done, all formal and by the book and shit.

He moved to the chair he'd been instructed to sit in.

Let's get this charade over with, he thought. *I got a New York strip waitin' with my name on it.*

The judge cleared his throat. "It says here you've been arrested for drug trafficking," Judge Landry said. He spoke articulately, but with a pronounced New Orleans accent.

He looked down on Marcus over his glasses, waiting for a response.

"That's what they done accused me of," he said, sitting back in the chair and crossing his arms. "Ain't true."

"Right," the judge said, all sarcastic.

"Whatever. You can't prove nothin'."

"I don't have to," the judge replied, slowly grinning. "It doesn't work that way, young man. Your guilt or innocence on that matter will be determined at your trial." The judge set the paper aside and picked up another, looking down at it through his reading glasses.

Finally, he looked down at Marcus again. "You've been brought in this morning to be informed that another charge has been added." He paused and gave Marcus a smile. "And I wanted to tell you myself, after which I will file a recusal, removing me from hearing your case."

Marcus sat up straight. "Added? What are you talking about?"

"Obstruction of justice, under Section 1503 of Title 18. A felony that will add ten years to your sentence when you're convicted."

"What? What are you talking about? I ain't done nothin'. I don't even know what that means."

The judge turned to the woman at a desk next to him and nodded.

She said, "Section 1503 of Title 18 defines obstruction of justice as an act that corruptly or by threats or force, or by any threatening letter or communication, influences, obstructs, or impedes, or endeavors to influence, obstruct, or impede, the due administration of justice."

"Huh?"

The judge removed his reading glasses and set them aside, his eyes boring holes in Marcus's. "It means you threatened the wrong judge."

He turned to the cop standing beside the bench. "Bailiff, remove this filthy excrement from my courtroom. He is to be remanded to Louisiana State Penitentiary without bail, awaiting arraignment in Judge Steele's court."

The State Pen? What the hell did JP go and do?

"But, sir!"

There was a mistake. This couldn't be right. He had contacts in the local jail, but upstate? Where the hell was JP?

The judge looked back down at him. "*Sir*, now, is it? Well, you'll be using that word a lot in the near future." A shitass grin spread across the judge's face as he glared down at Marcus. "I hope you have a pleasant stay in Angola, young man."

CHAPTER TWENTY-EIGHT

Charity and Enrique rode back from the airport in silence, taking an alternate route to avoid driving past the scene where the three cartel members had been slain.

"This organization you work for..." Enrique began. "What exactly is it?"

Charity looked over at him, studying his features. It was obvious he had an axe to grind against this cartel, and now that the leaders were dead, it would be up to people like him to keep them out of the idyllic little Mexican town on the beach.

"Armstrong is a research company," she said. "Primarily oil and oceanographic research."

He glanced over at her. "The Campeche shelf is already well-known. There are dozens of wells already."

"There's a part of the organization that researches *other* things," she said.

"I've heard the rumors."

"What do they say?" she asked, genuinely curious what the word on the street was.

"I've heard that if someone needs help... that is, some government agency... if they need help with something they cannot control themselves, they can call Armstrong Research."

"But you'd have to know who to call," Charity said. "Armstrong doesn't exactly advertise."

As the sky was just beginning to lighten with early dawn, Enrique pulled into the small lot at the pier and put the van in park. "The boat is gone."

Charity looked out over the anchorage and indeed, *MollySue* was nowhere in sight. She could see *Wind Dancer* and noted that her dinghy was tied to the stern. Someone, probably Harald Waalkens, had moved it for her before *MollySue* pulled anchor.

She opened her camera case, then removed the long lens and pressed the release. After she pulled the tray out, she handed Enrique a card. On it was nothing more than a telephone number.

"That's Armstrong's tip line," Charity told him, as she handed him the card. "Do you know what a confidential informant is?"

He grinned and nodded, accepting the card.

"You can call that number with information about any kind of criminal activity, day or night, seven days a week," Charity told him, "The first time you call with information, tell whoever answers that you are calling for Charity Styles. They'll ask you some inane question and no matter what it is, your answer is blue, okay?"

He nodded his head, slipping the card into his wallet. "Blue. Got it. What then?"

"You'll be given a code name and your number will be recorded," Charity replied. "After that, just identify yourself by the code name and whoever answers will know who you are and have any past information you provided at their fingertips." Charity's eyes drifted to *Sea Biscuit*, anchored sedately near where *MollySue* had been. "Who knows? It might even be Savannah who answers."

"This is what she does for Armstrong?"

"Sometimes," Charity replied wistfully. Then she turned back to

Enrique. "We obviously can't do missing cats or anything like that, but any information you provide will be linked to other intel from other sources and compiled. And when it's enough, some action will be taken. Usually, that's just turning it over to the authorities."

"And other times?" he asked, searching her eyes.

"Other times..." Charity replied, "it gets complicated."

"Will I ever see you again?"

She smiled at the young man. "You never know."

His dark eyes sparkled. "Until then, *Senorita* Styles."

"Thanks for all your help, Enrique," she said, pulling a folded banknote from a small pocket next to the cards.

She handing it to him.

"What is this?" he asked, unfolding the bill.

"That's ten thousand dollars in Brunei currency," she replied. "Worth about seventy-five hundred U.S."

"I cannot accept this," he said, extending it back to her. "That is more than a hundred thousand pesos, what most people in this town earn in a year!"

"Consider it a down payment," she replied, opening the door, and getting out. "Pay it forward, Enrique. That's all I ask. I'll see you around some time."

Charity closed the door and stood by the gate as Enrique drove away. The time had come for her to face Savannah.

Though she'd been thinking about this moment for months now, her mind was blank. She'd been up for more than twenty-four hours, with only a short nap.

All the gentle words she'd conjured, the phrases to explain herself, the apology for all the hurt, vanished into the morning air.

This feeling was new, and uncomfortable. Charity couldn't remember a time when she couldn't find the words to say what she wanted to say. Somehow, she would have to trust that the words would come. Because it had to be done.

Passing through the gate, she found a water taxi. The pilot was lying across three seats, his hat over his face, but rose quickly when Charity tapped on the gunwale.

Ten minutes later, she was back aboard *Wind Dancer*, and for a moment, the sedate familiarity made all her problems and worries drift away. But only for a moment.

Her phone trilled and she fished it out of her pocket. When she looked at the display, she grinned.

An Old Fart is Calling was displayed on the screen.

She pressed *Accept* and put the phone to her ear. "Good morning, Colonel."

"I got Savannah's M.A. message over an hour ago," Stockwell growled, meaning that Savannah had informed him that the mission had been accomplished.

Charity steeled herself for the reprimand she knew was coming for not reporting regularly.

"How'd she do?" he asked, his voice low.

"How did she... Wait. Is there something going on I don't know about, Colonel?"

"I knew it would just be a matter of time," he said. "The world's changed. There is danger everywhere."

"You knew she'd be in danger?"

"Sooner or later, I knew she'd have to ask Commander Livingston for help with something."

"And you put her in charge of this rescue," Charity said. "Why?"

Charity looked over toward *Sea Biscuit*. There were no lights on.

"In the hope that I could make her see what making a real life or death decision was all about."

"You bastard!"

There was silence for a moment. Then, Stockwell let out a heavy sigh. "I deserve that, Captain. But now, it's done. Her cherry's popped and it's time for her to get on with life. Let me know how it turns out."

"You really crossed a line here, Colonel," Charity said.

He said nothing, and when Charity glanced at the screen, she saw he'd ended the call.

"Son-of-a..." Charity hissed.

He'd intentionally put Savannah into a position where she would have to get her hands dirty.

That was low, even for Stockwell.

Charity went below and turned on the water heater before stripping out of her dirty clothes. It only took the ten-gallon tank a few minutes to heat up, and when she stepped into the small shower, she turned the hot water on full, steam billowing instantly. Then she shut it off and turned on the raw water nozzle, lathering up with cold saltwater, before blasting the soap away with the searing hot fresh water again.

When she stepped out of the shower, her skin was reddened. She dressed quickly, and afterward went to the galley for a quick breakfast of a banana and a protein bar—not her usual morning routine. Then she got into her dinghy and made her way to *Sea Biscuit*, with the sun shining on the right side of her face.

On approach to the stern, she looped the painter around the cleat, then killed the engine. Once she'd tied off, she stood in her dinghy and waited by the small swim platform.

"Good morning," she called out.

The scent of fresh biscuits wafted from the open hatch of the aft cabin, and Alberto scampered toward her on the side deck.

"Hey, Aunt Charity! Guess what?"

"I'm all out of guesses. You'll have to tell me." She glanced over his head, looking for Savannah. Usually Charity adored Alberto and his exuberant innocence, but this morning her nerves were on fire.

"The other day, I saw a dog on the beach, and he found a crab."

"No," she said, feigning disbelief.

"Yeah, and guess what?"

"What?"

"It bit him right on the nose."

"No way," Charity said, forcing a grin.

His face fell. "What's wrong?"

Couldn't fool this one. "Nothing, darling. I just need to talk to your mom. You know, grown-up stuff."

He shrugged. His life had been a constant stream of adult conversations that he knew he wasn't supposed to hear.

Savannah stepped out of the pilothouse on the starboard side. "Good morning," she said, as she wiped her hands on her apron—a cute red and blue one with an anchor and the words *Galley Wench* stenciled over her heart. No doubt a gift from Jesse.

"Breakfast is just about ready," Savannah said, walking back along the starboard side. "I was just checking the biscuits." She shrugged and wrung her hands again, then brushed them down her apron. "I've made enough for an army. Not sure why. I guess I felt like cooking this morning."

"Is everything all right?" Charity asked.

"Yeah, yeah," she said, brushing off the events of the previous night. "C'mon in."

Charity didn't think she could sit through breakfast before talking to Savannah; it was just too much to hold in.

She followed her friend down the port side to the salon hatch.

"I was hoping we could talk," Charity said hesitantly.

"Yeah, me too."

"Oh?"

She hadn't expected that. Savannah had been so distant, so detached. Was she ready to give Charity the admonishments she deserved?

After Savannah stepped down into the salon, she called out to Alberto on the foredeck. Charity moved past her as she waited by the hatch for him.

When he appeared, Savannah said, "Honey, go play on the upper deck until I call you for breakfast, okay?"

Alberto dutifully trotted up to the flybridge, leaving the two women alone.

Charity slid into the seat at the dinette, putting the table between her and Savannah.

She'd always hated having to talk. She'd seen the horrors of war, killed people, and had seen her comrades die on the battlefield. She'd had to face shrinks and superior officers, all of whom had the power to end her career, which they ultimately had.

All they ever wanted her to do was talk, talk, talk.

They wanted to know how the unspeakable ordeal and torment she'd experienced in Afghanistan had affected *her*.

But it was always the men *in her charge* that she'd lost who most haunted Charity's nightmares. All butchered by the Talibani with the scar on his face.

The shrinks never wanted her to talk about that. No one understood. Well, almost no one. Jesse and DJ knew her deepest, darkest secrets and thoughts. They knew the pain she'd experienced, as only someone who'd been there could.

The doctors and therapists had only wanted her to talk about what *they* thought she should talk about. She'd tried, really, she had. It wasn't a problem with the words. She just didn't want to relive it over and over again.

So every time she sat down with someone, she'd feel their eyes, their patient waiting, as if that would help. It just set her nerves buzzing. She'd rehashed it so many times, she was numb to it.

She often told a new shrink the full, graphic details in an opening monologue that lasted several minutes. After which, she'd smile and ask if that was what they'd wanted to hear.

One ran out of the room, hand clamped firmly over his mouth.

None of that made her as nervous as she was right then aboard *Sea Biscuit*.

"Savannah, I've been wanting to talk to you about—"

Savannah burst into tears. Her hands came up to cover her face.

"Oh, Charity. What have I done? I'm standing here trying to pretend nothing happened! To act and speak normally! But this whole thing is anything *but* normal!"

Charity started to push herself up from the seat. "What? What do you mean?"

Savannah plopped down next to her. "I don't know how you do it, how you live with it. And Jesse..."

Charity's gut clenched into a tight ball, and she swallowed hard, her throat suddenly going dry.

"I'm so sorry," she managed to croak out. "I didn't... I mean... I don't know what to say."

Oh God, I'm terrible at this.

"That man raised his gun," Savannah cried out in obvious torment. "He was going to shoot Poppy! There was no question in my mind, at least I can say that. I was certain he would've killed her. But immediately after, I started doubting everything."

238

Charity exhaled. "What are you talking about?"

The shooting?

"I mean, yeah," Charity stammered. "That's right. He most definitely was. You don't know the half of—"

"But I wasn't sure!" Savannah blurted out. "I mean, not fully and absolutely sure." She sobbed again. "But can you ever be sure of what's inside a man's heart?"

Jesse? Charity thought, having a hard time following what Savannah was trying to tell her.

"You made the right call," she said, sticking with what seemed to be troubling her friend the most at the moment.

Damn you, Stockwell! Charity thought. *She shouldn't have to deal with this on top of what I did.*

"How can you be so certain it was the right call?" Savannah asked, on the verge of hysteria. "The only person who could possibly answer that is dead!"

"They were after Agent McVie all along," Charity began.

"Huh?"

"Remember the proof-of-life picture? They were targeting Poppy, not us. Harper had heard them talk about a redhead while she was captive. And Poppy had put away one of their top men over on the West Coast. She was probably on a hit list."

"I don't understand," Savannah said, grabbing a paper towel and dabbing at the corners of her eyes.

"I forgot that you didn't hear that," Charity explained. "If you hadn't made the call, Poppy would be dead for sure. The man I shot had orders to kill her on sight."

"But I didn't know that at the time."

"Doesn't matter. Right call."

Savannah stared at Charity for a long moment. "Knowing that

doesn't change how I feel. I mean, it's just so... I had no idea. And all this time... Jesse, he... Oh, Charity." She leaned into her shoulder and sobbed.

Charity wrapped her arm around her friend. "It's okay. You're okay," was all she could think to say.

"It's not okay!" Savannah whisper-shouted, getting to her feet and listening to Alberto scooting around on the flybridge.

Savannah gazed back down at her with sad eyes. "A man is dead, and it's on me. I made the call. His blood is on my hands."

Charity reached for another paper towel and handed it to Savannah. "No. That man made a choice. He was going to take a life, so that made his life forfeit. That's how it works. Personal responsibility. His blood is wholly on his own hands."

"You make it sound so simple."

Charity stared into her friend's eyes, then pulled her back down beside her. "It is *just* that simple, Savvy. I've known you for a long time. You're a good person. That man chose. He lost."

She shook her head. "But maybe he was—"

"There are no maybes," Charity stated firmly. "There are only facts. You were in a real-world combat situation. He drew a weapon. There's only one appropriate response to that. Neutralize the threat."

Savannah blew her nose. "I don't know, Charity. Maybe he was just going to threaten her, like verbally. Maybe he wouldn't have pulled the trigger."

"Okay, maybe. If you need to think of it that way. But in that situation, the response is still the same, because we don't take those kinds of chances. The lives of good people can't hang on a maybe. We neutralize the threat, just like you and I did on Hoffman's."

Savannah looked up sharply, her eyes searching Charity's as

both women recalled the men who'd attacked them there.

"Poppy's life was in jeopardy," Charity said. "We now know she was marked for execution. You made the right call. It's what I would have done. It's what *Jesse* would have done."

Savannah's eyes fixed on Charity's, and she burst into tears again.

Oh no, that was the wrong thing to say.

"Don't you believe me?" Charity said.

Savannah shook her head. "No. Yes. I mean." She blew her nose again. "It's just, here I've been, skulking about like a child, running away from the man I love because... because I didn't understand. But now. I just don't know. I knew all the stories about him when I married him. I saw him in action against three bigger men. He'd told me of his nightmares, about the ghosts of those he'd killed haunting him." She sniffed and looked deeply into Charity's eyes. "I know you have them too. How do you continue on?"

"Well..." Charity drew in a breath to steady herself. "That's what I've been wanting to talk to you about. The night you left—"

"You mean the night I ran away, because that's what this has been. What a naive fool I've been."

Charity shook her head, still confused. Savannah wasn't making any sense, tacking back and forth.

She took Savannah's shoulders in her hands. "You had every right to be upset."

"No, I should've trusted Jesse to make that call," Savannah exclaimed, shaking her head. "Like Poppy trusted me to make it last night. You just don't know what it's really like until you've been in that situation, do you? And I know he's had to make a call like that many, many times. Like you. He handles it like a professional. And I was *judging* him. I mean, it just seemed, at the time, that there was

WAYNE STINNETT AND KIMBERLI A. BINDSCHATEL

no justification for you and him to kill those two men."

Charity sat back and looked at her friend. Had this been the reason she'd left? Not because of what had happened in front of the police with Charity? But that couldn't be. Then she remembered that Savannah hadn't heard the conversation Chyrel had tapped into.

"Savannah," she said softly, "you didn't hear the threats Paladin made in an intercepted phone call. Jesse was in the right."

"What threats?"

"You'd left the comm shack that night," Charity explained. "To make dinner for Alberto. We were making our way to shore and while you were gone, Chyrel intercepted a call Paladin was making to that Orion guy. He used a lot of racial slurs and promised to kill again."

Savannah stared at her and slowly nodded, connecting the dots and finally understanding.

Then the tears came again, full force. She leaned her head on Charity's shoulder. Charity pulled her into an embrace and stroked her hair.

So, she didn't leave because of me?

Charity remembered something her dad had said many years ago.

"It's not always about you."

Was it possible that her own feelings of guilt, of being liable for the breakup, had clouded her assessment of Savannah's motives?

Savannah would know that what Charity had done was the right thing to do in that situation to throw off the police. She might have improvised the same thing, if she'd been the one on the op with Jesse.

Now she felt like a fool. She had been on the verge of admitting

242

her feelings for Jesse.

Totally selfish, she thought.

She'd just be dumping all of her emotional baggage on Savannah, and for what? To make herself feel better?

She knew she had some new emotions to sort out. And she would. She knew now that it was for her to deal with on her own, as long as she never crossed that line.

She vowed right then and there, as she held Savannah in her arms, that she would never, ever even get close to that line again.

As Savannah's sobs began to recede, she sat upright and looked into Charity's eyes. "I need to call him right away."

Charity nodded.

"But what did you want to talk about?"

"What? I..."

"You said you wanted to talk to me."

"Oh, I—"

The smoke alarm went off, its loud trill making both of them sit back with a start.

"Oh crap, the biscuits!"

Savannah jumped up and rushed to the oven. She flung the door open and, using the corner of her apron, yanked out a pan of black biscuits. She dumped the pan into the sink with a clatter, then turned on the water, dousing them.

Slowly, Savannah turned toward Charity and shrugged meekly. "I guess maybe I should stick to spy work."

They both burst into laughter.

Running footsteps could be heard on the side deck, then Alberto knelt in front of the door, a small fire extinguisher, probably from the anchor chain locker, in his hands. "What happened?"

"I burned the biscuits," Savannah said, laughing and dabbing at her eyes with the top of her apron. "There's no fire."

"Ya don't have to cry about it," he said, stepping down into the cabin and looking confused.

"I saw a nice little breakfast place on the beach," Charity said. "Let's go there, my treat."

"Sounds good," Savannah replied with a smile. "Right after I call Jesse."

"Mom?"

Savannah nodded at Alberto. "I think it's time we go home, son."

THE END

WAYNE'S AFTERWORD

I'd first like to thank Kim for collaborating with me on this book. It was a lot of fun, and about halfway through, she and her husband, Ken, found their way to our little Sea Islands in their RV, and we sat out on the patio and went over what we had up to that point and came up with some great ideas for the last half.

Special thanks to my core readers, Mike Ramsey, Drew Mutch, Deg Priest, Kim DeWitt, Thomas Crisp, Debbie Kocol, Charles Höfbauer, Dana Vihlen, Katy McKnight, Alan Fader, and Jason Hebert, who continue to amaze me with their attention to the little details.

I owe more thanks to my family, especially my wife, Greta, than I could ever possibly express. Greta is a constant source of ideas and a wonderful sounding board. Our kids are a constant support and, though they don't always realize it, some of my best ideas come from their mouths.

A special thanks to Jordan, our youngest, who not only runs the online *Gaspar's Revenge* Ship's Store, but also handles most of the technical side of my business, including being the producer of my livestream, *TalkWrite*. Subscribe on YouTube, and don't forget to click the Notification bell to get word when we go live with our guests.

If you're not subscribed to my newsletter, you should do that, too. Subscribers get discounts on everything from eBooks and audiobooks to T-shirts and coffee mugs, and Jordan recently added some new swag. And we have fruit-juicy tropical shirts coming up on the horizon. So, keep a weather eye out for new *Gaspar's Revenge* and Rusty Anchor bootie to be added to the store.

My team of professionals at Aurora Publicity are to be commended for all the work they put in; from cover design and formatting to uploading to dozens of retail outlets, they always get it done and on time.

I count the legendary and multi-talented Nick Sullivan as part of the team. He goes way beyond being the voice of Jesse and crew, often being called on for character input during the writing process. In the eight years that he's been recording my audiobooks, we've become very good friends. In fact, Nick is my co-host on *TalkWrite*. He's also become a great tropical storyteller—don't miss his *Deep Series*.

Marsha Zinberg has the first critical look at my manuscripts after my team of core readers. They only look for plot holes and red herrings. Marsha has decades of experience as a professional editor and she's the reason my stories can be turned into novels. I've learned so much about writing from her over these last four years.

Thanks also to my final proofreader, Donna Rich. After dozens have read and worked on the manuscript, including my reading it at least four times, Donna always finds a handful of errors.

During the writing of this novel, I became a great-grandfather. On April 5, 2023, the first boy-child in three generations was born to my family. Malakai Tomas Stinnett arrived about ten minutes before I got to the hospital, following a six-hour drive down I-95. Since then, he's barely raised his voice. With his mom, two aunts, and his grandma all right there at his beck and call, he doesn't need to.

Welcome to Earth, Kai. I look forward to showing some of it to you one day.

KIM'S AFTERWORD

Thank you, Wayne, for believing in me and getting me back to my writing desk. It was fun to hang out with Charity again, and bringing Poppy along was an added joy.

An additional THANK YOU to all those Wayne has thanked above. He's put together quite a team, and it was an honor to be invited along.

Sometimes, even we writers need to get out and work with other people, jump start the creative process, and simply enjoy the company of other human beings. Since the pandemic, I've become somewhat of a hermit—not just in physical space, but in pulling away from the writing world as well. This was my way of dipping my toe back in.

Special thanks to my husband, Ken, for nudging me in that direction too. We shall see where it takes me next.

And a big shout out to all of you who read our books and take the time, even if just for a moment, to consider how we impact our natural world, especially the animals with which we share this planet. Every thought, every gesture, every passing-along of information makes a difference, no matter how small. Thank you for helping me give voice to those who don't have one of their own.

If you'd like to receive my newsletter, please sign up on my website.

WWW.WAYNESTINNETT.COM.

Once a month, I'll bring you insights into my private life and writing habits, with updates on what I'm working on, special deals I hear about, and new books by other authors that I'm reading.

The Jerry Snyder Caribbean Mystery Series

Wayward Sons

The Charity Styles Caribbean Thriller Series

Merciless Charity
Ruthless Charity
Reckless Charity
Enduring Charity

Enduring Charity
Vigilant Charity
Lost Charity
Elusive Charity
Forced Charity

The Jesse McDermitt Caribbean Adventure Series

Fallen Out
Fallen Palm
Fallen Hunter
Fallen Pride
Fallen Mangrove
Fallen King
Fallen Honor
Fallen Tide
Fallen Angel
Fallen Hero
Rising Storm
Rising Fury

Rising Force
Rising Charity
Rising Water
Rising Spirit
Rising Thunder
Rising Warrior
Rising Moon
Rising Tide
Steady As She Goes
All Ahead Full
Man Overboard
Cast Off
Fish On!

Non Fiction

Blue Collar to No Collar

No Collar to Tank Top

Also By Kimberli A. Bindschatel

Operation Tropical Affair   Operation Artic Deception
Operation Orca Rescue   Operation Dolphin Spirit
Operation Grizzly Camp   Operation Wolf Pack
Operation Turtle Ransom   The Path to the Sun

You can find Kimberli at
WWW.KIMBERLIBINDSCHATEL.COM

The Gaspar's Revenge Ship's Store is open.

There, you can purchase all kinds of swag
related to my books. You can find it at

WWW.GASPARS-REVENGE.COM

Made in the USA
Las Vegas, NV
31 January 2024

85138250R00144